Isle of Stars
The Isle Chronicles Book 3

Wayne Thomas Batson

Spearhead Publishing

Baltimore, New York, Seattle

Wayne Thomas Batson at Spearhead Publishing
www.enterthedoorwithin.blogspot.com

Publisher's Note: This is a work of fiction. Names, characters, places, and incidents are a product of the author's imagination. Locales and public names are sometimes used for atmospheric purposes. Any resemblance to actual people, living or dead, or to businesses, companies, events, institutions, or locales is completely coincidental.

Editing by Laura G. Johnson of Red Pen Proofreading

Book Layout © 2014 BookDesignTemplates.com

Cover Main Artwork: Caleb Havertape Illustration
Cover Design and Layout: Wayne Thomas Batson

Isle of Stars / Wayne Thomas Batson. -- 1st ed.
ISBN –Pending

DEDICATION:

To the Maker of the Stars for moving heaven and earth to rescue a swarthy, pirate rogue like me, I sail for you, forever.

"These things—the beauty, the memory of our own past—are good images of what we really desire; but if they are mistaken for the thing itself they turn into dumb idols, breaking the hearts of their worshipers. For they are not the thing itself; they are only the scent of a flower we have not found, the echo of a tune we have not heard, news from a country we have never yet visited."

C.S. LEWIS, THE WEIGHT OF GLORY

Author's Foreword

As a fantasy/adventure author of 16+ novels and counting, I've written some pretty strange tales. *Weird* comes with the territory, right? But I must confess, this story might just be the strangest of all. For those who are unaware, this story is part of a tradition of Christmas Fan-Request Stories. Each year, I post a public poll on my website (www.enterthedoorwithin.blogspot.com) and give readers a chance to vote for the story concept they would most like to see written as a Christmas Gift.

This year, there was a bit of a goof in the results, meaning I goofed, actually. And so, the resulting story has taken on a rather bizarre turn. Initially, the story was just going to be a straight-up *Isle Chronicles* pirate adventure. But, in order to satisfy the desires of my wonderful (and slightly loony) readers, the story has also become a kind of experiment.

Readers expecting the pirate action to begin straight away, will be surprised to find none other than Kaylie Keaton from the *Dreamtreaders* series opening the story in the prologue. You will also note cameos from characters from all over the Batson book catalogue: *The Door Within Trilogy, The Berinfell Prophecies, The Dark Sea Annals*—even *The Misadventures of Strylun and Xerk*. But fear not, there's still a serious story to be told here. Perhaps, more than one. But I'll leave that for you, the readers, to discover on your own.

Merry Christmas, and until next time,
Never alone, Endurance and Victory, Hold Fast, and Anchor First, Anchor Deep!

-Wayne Thomas Batson, Christmas 2015

Table of Contents:

Prologue, Page 1

Chapter 1: Wedding Bells are a' Cracking, Page 6

Chapter 2: Unexpected Cargo, Page 13

Chapter 3: Stories and Stowaways, Page 19

Chapter 4: Shark Attack, Page 27

Chapter 5: Turning the Tables, Page 33

Chapter 6: Questions, Page 36

Chapter 7: Lakeba Island, Page 45

Chapter 8: Father Carroll, Page 50

Chapter 9: The Broken Spyglass, Page 56

Chapter 10: Aboard the Red Corsair, Page 62

Chapter 11: Isle of Stars, Page 67

Chapter 12: The Chase, Page 73

Chapter 13: The Climb, Page 81

Chapter 14: The Cave, Page 85

Chapter 15: In the Midst of Red Light, Page 91

Chapter 16: Roses and Thornes, Page 97

Chapter 17: A Starry Trail to Follow, Page 104

Chapter 18: The Fear of God, Page 108

Chapter 19: Broken Things, Page 112

Chapter 20: Brits, Brides, and Brigantines, Page 121

Epilogue, Page 130

About the Author, Page 135

Acknowledgments, Page 137

Become a Patron, Page 143

Other Books by Wayne Thomas Batson, Page 144

PROLOGUE

"You've got a lot of books for a nine-year-old, yep." Amy Pitsitakis pushed round-framed glasses up the bridge of her nose. Her owlish green eyes sparkled with something close to envy as she edged along the vast bookcase in her young friend's room. "And to think...people sometimes call *me* a bookworm."

Kaylie Keaton laughed, freckles dancing on her cheeks. She sat on the edge of her bed and bounced a stuffed scarecrow doll on her knee. "Bookworm," she sniggered. "That's not a very nice thing to say, is it, Mr. Patches?" Kaylie nodded her scarecrow doll in agreement. Then she raised an eyebrow. "Did you know the term bookworm comes from the larvae of the varied carpet beetle? *Anthrenus verbasci*, the carpet beetle larva will often feed on older books that used starches and proteins in their binding materials."

"I sure didn't know that." Amy said. "Nope."

"We currently use much different binding materials," Kaylie said. "So we don't have to worry about modern books getting munched. And ebooks are safest of all." She giggled. "But I still like paper books."

"Me too," Amy agreed. "I might have to come raid your collection. What do you recommend?"

Kaylie laid Patches on the bed and then bounced down to scour her bookcase. As she roamed to and fro, sliding her index finger across the spines of row upon row of books, Kaylie made all sorts of faces and sounds. Delighted grins, hilarious snorts, inquisitive smirks, loving sighs, and highly irritated scowls—it was as if she was reliving flashes of each novel as she touched them.

"I'm torn," she said finally.

"How so?" Amy asked.

"Well, I really like the novels by this Batson guy, but I'm still mad at him, so I'm not sure I can recommend his books."

"You're mad? At…an author?" Amy laughed. "Why?"

Kaylie browsed her shelves, stopped, and yanked out a dark blue book. "Here it is," she said. "Isle of Fire. It's from his Isle Chronicles pirate adventures. It was such a great story but—"

"Don't tell me," Amy said. "The author killed off one of your favorite characters?"

Kaylie shook her head. "No, no…I'd hunt him down and kick him in the shins if he did that."

"Were there spelling errors?"

"No. Not that either."

"Wait, I know. It had a stupid ending, didn't it?"

Kaylie frowned. "Not so much a stupid ending, just vexing. The story concludes with thrills galore, but there's a gigantic thread left dangling at the very end. I was so angry I flung the book across the room."

"Have you considered seeing someone about your violent responses to fiction?"

Kaylie rolled her eyes. "My book-tossing incident was fully warranted," she said. "You'll see if you read it."

"I do like pirate stories," Amy said, scowling and holding up a finger in the shape of a hook. "Arrr!"

Kaylie rolled her eye and plucked another novel off her shelf. This one had a fiery red colored binding. "You'll want to have this one, Isle of Swords. It's the first book. Isle of Fire is book two. Read them in order, but don't say I didn't warn you." She handed both books to Amy and let out an audible growl.

"You're that upset?" Amy asked. "Over a little suspense?"

Kaylie turned beet red. "It is not a little suspense. It's more like an atomic suspense bomb!"

"Why not just read the third book?"

Kaylie shrieked, "That's just it! There isn't a third book! He just quit the series and wrote other stories."

"That is a little odd."

"What kind of sadistic nutball writes a duology anyway?" Red pigtails bouncing, Kaylie paced her room. "But, go ahead, read them, if you dare."

"I have to, now," Amy said. "Just to find out what you're fussing about."

Kaylie flounced onto her bed and snuggled up with Patches.

Amy scanned the back of each book, muttering to herself. After a few moments, she asked, "How's Dreamtreading?"

"Fun," Kaylie replied. "Not too much work since, well, you know."

Amy nodded thoughtfully. "Have you learned anything new about your will? Any new power?"

Kaylie nodded vigorously. "Every time I go," she said. "Just last week, I learned how to stitch up a Dream breach with just one stroke. Gabe says he's never seen anything like it."

"Cool," Amy replied. "Bet Archer's jealous."

"Archer's jealous of what?" Archer stood at Kaylie's door. Beneath a mantle of very red hair, his dark green eyes smoldered with mock suspicion. "What are you two up to this time?"

"Nothing," Kaylie said, shrugging. "Amy was just saying you'd be jealous of my Dreamtreading powers."

"Oh, that," he said. "Nah. Not jealous. Kaylie's been smarter than me since she was seven. I'm used to it. Now, it's more a feeling of awe, really. Besides, there are some benefits for me. With all that power, Kaylie gets to do more work in the Dream." He turned to leave but paused to say, "Amy, are you going to come back downstairs anytime soon? We've got a boatload of A.P. Physics to study."

"A.P. Physics?" Kaylie mused. "Lucky! Ah, I can't wait until high school."

"It'll be here soon enough," Amy said, giving Kaylie's shoulder a friendly squeeze. "But some of us need to actually study to get good grades, so I'd better go. I mean…so that I can help Archer."

Archer frowned. "Hey!"

"Just kidding," Amy said with a coy twirl of her white-blond hair and a clandestine wink to Kaylie.

Kaylie waved to Archer and winked back at Amy. When they were gone, Kaylie shut the door and went right to her closet. Beneath a colorful pile of fuzzy towels on the lowest shelf, Kaylie removed a rather large book. Inside the front cover, tucked into a carefully woven pocket, was a very long white feather. Talking about Batson and his confounded two-book pirate series had given Kaylie the inkling of an idea.

She removed the Summoning Feather, as it was called, and tapped its gossamer fletching against her chin. "I wonder," she mumbled, glancing at the empty spaces on her bookshelf where Isle of Swords and Isle of Fire had resided. "I'm sure it couldn't hurt."

Kaylie tossed the white feather into the air. It vanished in a comet-trail of blue and purple sparkles.

"Kaylie Keaton," came a stern voice from the sparkles. "This had better be important."

Kaylie clapped as Master Gabriel, the leader of the Dreamtreader Order, twinkled into existence. He was twice as tall as Kaylie and broad as a barn door. He wore armor of some gray metal that glimmered blue or white depending on the way he turned. A long gray cloak cascaded down from his shoulders and almost totally hid the hilt of the massive sword at his side. "I do have other tasks," he said gruffly, "besides catering to the needs of a little girl. What is it this time? You'd like me to fetch you a drink of water?"

"You're funny, Gabe," Kaylie said, shaking her head. "No, I want to do some Dreamtreading tonight."

Master Gabriel raised a bushy eyebrow. "But you are not on duty tonight. Nick should have things covered."

"That's even better," Kaylie said.

"What do you mean?"

"I want to practice," she said. "If Nick's covering all the breaches tonight, I'll be able work undisturbed."

Master Gabriel cleared his throat. "Work on what?"

"I have some ideas," Kaylie said.

"Those are rather famous last words," Master Gabriel replied, his dark, deep-set eyes flashing.

"Don't be so stuffy," she said. "You told me whenever I feel my will growing stronger, that I need to exercise. You told me to keep pushing my limits. That's what I want to practice."

Master Gabriel looked sharply to the ceiling. "Why do I get the feeling I'm going to regret this?"

"Don't worry," Kaylie said. "I'll be fine."

"Those," Master Gabriel muttered, "are also famous last words."

"C'mon, Gabe," Kaylie giggled, "what could possibly go wrong?"

"You've outdone yourself this time," Master Gabriel replied, his armor flashing incandescent light. "For *those* are at the very top of the list...of famous last words."

CHAPTER ONE

WEDDING BELLS ARE A' CRACKING

"Where are they?" Anne Ross demanded as she frantically raced across the broad, sun-bleached deck of the three-masted Portuguese man-of-war, *The Robert Bruce*. Anne's long red hair flailed behind her like a fiery comet trail, and her hazel eyes smoldered with barely restrained fury. She skidded to a halt near the main mast, put her hands on her hips, and bellowed, "Have you all lost your minds? Or just your will? Won't someone answer me?"

A shadow fell upon her as if the sun, high in the South Pacific sky overhead, had suddenly been blotted out by a rogue bank of cloud. A voice boomed from behind her, "What seems to be the problem, Red?"

Anne spun on her heels. "Oooh, Jules! How many times do I have to tell you, don't call me that!"

Jules raised a bristly eyebrow, an expression that, with his dark skin made his eye seem like a searchlight. "I beg forgiveness," the man-mountain replied. He gave a half bow, the gesture highlighting how massive his cannonball shoulders actually were. "You see, I was distracted by your beguiling crimson hair. You cannot blame a man for that, can you? Ask your husband-to-be." His laughter was a deep and hearty blast of thunder.

But Anne wasn't laughing. She wasn't even smiling.

"That's just it!" she berated him. "If I'm to have a husband…if I'm to even have a proper wedding, then things cannot just disappear when I need them."

"Something's gone missing, has it?" Jules cracked the knuckles on his ham-sized fists. "What scoundrel has made off with, er…what is it you're missing exactly?"

"The wreaths, of course!" she practically howled. "And the garlands? I packed the crate myself and saw to it that Jacques St. Pierre stowed the crate just outside the forecastle cabins. Now, it's gone! You can't expect a girl to have a proper Christmas season wedding without wreaths and garlands, can you?"

Jules scratched at his scalp beneath the hem of the black skullcap he always wore. "Is this a trick question?"

"Oooooh!" Anne's complexion burned red. "It was a crate, a great, big crate." She pointed to the cabin doors built into the forecastle. "It was right there!"

"Oh!" Jules grunted, his bristly black mustache curling in an exultant smile. "You mean *that* crate! Red Eye took it down to the hold."

"Why would he take my garlands down below?" Anne muttered angrily. "How can he not know what a mess he's making of my wedding day?"

Jules put a reassuring hand on her shoulder, but she shrugged it off. Jules frowned. "Aren't you taking this a little too hard?" he asked. "The crate you need is in the hold. I can go get it. It's no trouble at—"

"No," Anne said with finality, "you will not get the crate. Red Eye will. Now, where is that scalawag?"

"It's about time for lunch," Jules replied. "Check the galley."

In a scarlet-faced huff, Anne raced toward the hatch. She stopped short a minute, spying a single-masted cutter racing across the harbor toward *The Robert Bruce*. "Da!" she hollered, knowing the Scottish endearment for Dad would get his attention. She pointed out to the water. "Looks like we've got company."

"I see it!" Declan Ross called down from the quarterdeck where he stood at the ship's wheel. Coppery eyebrows, mustache, and beard—all lit by the dazzling midday sun, burnished the rugged face of *The Bruce's* captain. He raised a spyglass. "By the thirty-nine lashes, plus one. That's Musketoon MacCready. What's he doing here? I didn't invite him to the wedding. You, Stede?"

"No, mon," Stede replied, stepping out from behind Ross and leaning at the rail. "But it be just like d'mon to crash d'party. I'll see to 'um." Ross's quartermaster and best friend clapped his massive hands together. "I'll see to 'um, all right, all right."

"No threat, Da?" Anne called.

"MacCready's no threat," Ross replied with a mischievous wink. "A pest...but not a threat." He took a second look through his spyglass. "He does seem to be in a blasted hurry to get here. But nothing I can't handle, my daughter."

"Good," Anne grumbled, leaping the trim on the hatch and thudding down the steps. "I have no time for this. I have no time for any of this."

The galley hummed, as busy as it could be. Being in port meant provisions overflowing, and Nubby, *The Bruce's* cook and in-a-pinch surgeon, was working triple-time to make sure the crew had plenty to eat. Anne found Red Eye at the slanting table on the port side of the galley. A crowd of men—deckhands, cannoneers, stewards, and powder monkeys—surrounded Red Eye who seemed engaged in the delivery of some flamboyant and tasteless tale.

Some things never change, Anne thought, drawing near and rolling her eyes. She'd heard him tell this particularly unsavory joke a hundred times, and she had no time for the hundred and first. "Red Eye!" she growled. "Why on earth did you put my garlands down in the hold?"

Red Eye didn't look up but, as if to block her intrusion, held up a hand and went on with his story. "Long ago, a captain by the name of Xerk Felmark and the crew of his Brit ship were in danger of being boarded by a nasty band of Spanish pirates. As the crew became frantic, Cap'n Felmark bellowed to his bosun, 'Bring me my red shirt!'

"The bosun quickly retrieved the captain's red shirt. Cap'n Felmark put it on in a flash and led the crew to battle the pirate boarding party. Although they lost a few lads, Cap'n Felmark and his men managed to drive off the scurvy invaders."

"Red Eye!" Anne shouted. "Need I remind you that I have a wedding to attend in four hours—my wedding!"

But, anxious to hear the rest of the story, the men around Red Eye crowded in tighter, effectively closing Anne out.

"Later that same week," Red Eye continued, "the lookout up in the crow's nest screamed that there were two pirate vessels sending boarding parties. This time, they were Turkish marauders. The crew cowered in fear, but Cap'n Felmark, calm as ever, shouted, 'Bring me my red shirt!'

"Garbed once more in his red shirt, Cap'n Felmark led his crew and, after a fierce battle, they managed to repel both boarding parties, although this time, there were more than a few dead and—"

"Red Eye!" Anne shouted.

"Shhhh!" The men glared at Anne. "This is the best part."

The storyteller, his blind eye blood red and gleaming with the flickering flame of the oil lantern hanging overhead, grinned and went on. "Weary from the fighting, the men sat around on deck that night recounting the battle when the bosun could contain his curiosity no longer. He turned to Cap'n Felmark and asked, 'Sir, why do you call for your red shirt before the battle?'

"Well, now, Cap'n Felmark, he gives the bosun a knowing look and says, 'If the battle is like to be fierce, I might be wounded. The red shirt hides the blood, and you men will continue to fight with courage.' And for such a thing, the crew loved their captain all the more."

"As dawn came the next morning, the lookout 'bout fell out of the crow's nest, so frantic was he, fair shrieking that ten ships were approaching, each one teeming with the cannibal pirates of the West Indies. I tell ye, there's never been a more screamin' mad bunch of cutthroats."

The galley had become silent as the men waited in rapt attention for Red Eye to finish. Anne shook with frustration but figured there was nothing more she could do without inciting a mutiny.

Red Eye lowered his voice and went on, "The crew were frightened but they didn't falter. They looked to Cap'n Felmark for his usual command. The captain, calm as ever, bellowed, 'Bring me my brown pants!'"

Plates rattled and food flew as the galley erupted in feverish bursts of laughter. One of the deckhands, a handsome but oddly pale man named Kearn, yanked Anne's elbow and crowed, "Did ye hear that? He wanted his brown pants! That means—"

"I know very well what that means!" Anne jerked away from him and plowed through the crowd. She shoved another sailor out of her way and crashed onto the bench nearest Red Eye. She brought her face so close to his that she could actually watch the dark red pupil grow in the midst of that dreadful, sickly pink orb of an eye.

"What..." Red Eye swallowed, "seems to be the trouble?"

"My wreaths and garlands!" Anne growled. "I need them topside. I had them topside, but you put them down in the hold."

Red Eye ran a finger along a ridge of scars on the left side of his face. Then, he gave a kind of snort-cough, "Oh, you mean the crate I put away? That what you need?"

Anne's blood boiling, her words escaped like wisps of steam, "Yes, that crate...is what I need. And I would be most heartily...pleased...if you would retrieve it from the hold and...return it to the main deck."

Red Eye slid like an eel away from the table and shouted over his shoulder, "I'll get right to it, then."

Anne stood, avoided the stunned gazes of the crowd, and brushed her blouse with her hands. "Now, if you'll all excuse me," she said, "I'll—"

"Look who it is!" Nubby shouted from the galley's serving line. With his one good hand, he waved a long ladle in the air. "If it isn't the bride-to-be, Anne Ross herself. Can I get ye anything? I've made me world famous iguana stew!"

"No, thank you," she replied curtly, storming toward the stairs. "Now, I need to find my future husband. Besides, I rather hate iguana stew."

CHAPTER TWO

UNEXPECTED CARGO

"I, Griffin Thorne, take you, Anne Ross, to be my lawfully wedded…" Cat's words trailed off. He'd seen something startling in the reflection of his cabin mirror. He'd seen his father.

And for a lightning-strike moment, there he was, Bartholomew Thorne. Alive again. Cold blue eyes stared back from the glass. Splinters of vengeful blue shone between the crusted, red-rimmed lids, from behind twisted strings of gray hair that swung like so many pale nooses from beneath his tricorn hat.

It wasn't the accusation in those eyes that disturbed Cat so much. It wasn't the knowing sneer or any of his father's other severe features. It was the presence of this visage…at all.

"You are dead," Cat whispered.

No, an ice-cracking, raspy voice said. *I am alive…in you.*

"No," Cat whispered. "By the grace of almighty God, there is no room for you within me. Begone with you, old man. The new man has come."

Like spirits of steam receding from a tropical lagoon, the vision left the glass. Cat saw himself: his own steady hazel eyes, his own meticulously groomed golden-brown sideburns jutting down from his eternally tousled blond hair. He straightened the ruffled white cravat that hung down several inches over the collar of his dark green waistcoat. "Well," he sighed. "I certainly look the part of husband. Now, if only I can live up to the privilege."

There came a splintering sharp rap upon the door and an urgent voice, "Cat!"

Before Cat could reach the knob, the door swung open. Captain Ross stepped in with his quartermaster, Stede, behind him. "I am afraid I bear bad news," Ross said.

"What is it this time?" Cat asked in jest. "Anne murder her seamstress? No? Wait, then. She's thrown Nubby overboard, has she?"

There was no mirth in Declan Ross's gray eyes. In fact, Cat thought, the captain wore a very particular expression, one usually reserved for a chase at sea. Ferocity etched itself into the furrows of his coppery brow, grim determination in the set of his jaw, and the slightest hint of mischief in one corner of his mouth—it all spoke plainly: the Sea Wolf was spoiling for the hunt.

Cat's shoulders fell. "Anne's not going to like this, is she?"

"No," Ross replied. "No, she will not. Nor you."

"Anne won't like what?" The voice was Anne's own, and she careened out of the hall, past Stede, to square up with her father. "What won't I like?"

The ferocity in Declan Ross's expression melted into a conflicted sigh. "The wedding, Anne," he said. "I'm sorry, but the wedding is off."

* * * * * * *

Kaylie Keaton skinned her knee on something rigid. She reached down and plucked out a splinter. Then she froze. Something was dreadfully wrong. No, that wasn't quite accurate. It wasn't so much that one thing was wrong, but rather, nothing at all was right.

It was pitch dark, but there were sounds…and smells. There was a deep rushing all around, punctuated by intermittent slaps. And there were all manner of creaks and groans as if Kaylie was surrounded by old wood under stress. She smelled salt and spices and something rather foul that reminded her of her father's old tackle box where little bits of bait and fish had rotted away, leaving nothing but a dull odor behind.

"What have I done?" Kaylie muttered. One moment she was experimenting with her will in an unpopulated canyon in Westmurk, one of her favorite territories in the Pattern District of the Dream. The next…well, she wasn't sure. Dreamtreading was always full of surprises. After all, anything can happen in a dream. *Still,* she thought, *I don't like the dark.* She reached for her will, the inner imaginative power of the mind harnessed by Dreamtreaders, and found nothing.

Alarm freezing a wicked trail across her shoulders, Kaylie tried again but couldn't produce even so much as a spark of light. There was nothing there. Her Dreamtreader will was drained. No, worse than that. It was altogether gone. "No, no, no," she muttered, fighting the panic welling up within her. She tried to stand but found a low ceiling of some thick material. She skidded backward, banging smartly into something hard. Then she tripped over something else and landed with a thump on her rump.

"Hey, this is my spot," came an indignant whisper at her side. "You kin' hide anywheres else you want, 'kay? Just not here."

Kaylie stared into the shadows and found the silhouette of a person crouching just inches away. A boy, likely, given the voice. She could hear his rapid breathing. "Who are you?" she asked.

"Nathaniel Hopper Blake," the silhouette replied.

A hand brushed Kaylie's shoulder, and she realized the lad was offering a friendly handshake. Tentatively, she took his hand and shook.

"I'm Kaylie Keaton," she said. "It's nice to meet you, Nathaniel. But can you—"

"No one calls me that," he interjected amiably.

"Oh," Kaylie replied. "Well, Blake…then?"

"Nope," he said. "Call me Hopper."

"Hopper," she repeated, chewing on something half-remembered. "Right. Well, Hopper, can you tell me where we are?"

"That's easy, Miss," he said. "You're aboard *The Robert Bruce*, captained by Declan Ross, it is. And we're moored in the South Pacific, just offin' the coast a' Santa Isabel Island."

"Santa Isabel?" Kaylie echoed. "That's one of the Solomon Islands." Her thoughts swam. *Declan Ross…The Robert Bruce? And…and…Hopper!* At that moment, she knew what she'd done. *It all makes sense now,* she thought. Or, at least it sort of made sense. She'd been fuming about the lack of a book after *Isle of Swords* and *Isle of Fire*, and she'd been experimenting with her will in the Dream. She'd felt a surge of power—no, not just a surge. It was more like a tidal wave of new power, and then everything had gone black. And now, here she was, but it wasn't text on pages in a book. It…was real. Worse still, this—this cosmic mistake—had somehow drained her Dreamtreading will. She had no power to call on. That led to one haunting thought: *how do I get back?*

"So, you stowing away too?" Hopper asked. "It's okay…iffn' you want. I know the folks here. They're right nice, but…they might put you to work."

Kaylie was about to respond when something skittered across the top of her shoe. "Hopper!" Kaylie whispered urgently. "There's something moving down around my ankles, but I can't see what it is! We need more light. Help me push!"

Hopper and Kaylie pushed as hard as they could on the low ceiling. It was some kind of heavy material, a tarp or maybe some kind of matting. Whatever it was, it moved just a few inches to the side, revealing a blade of light.

"Come on, push harder!" Kaylie shouted, feeling the skittering movements of something still at her feet. "Ewww, I don't think I'm going to like what this is! Push!"

They strained together, and the heavy material sideways, letting in more light, just enough to see the thing scurrying at Kaylie's feet.

"It's a rat," Hopper said. "Nifty, that."

Kaylie screamed.

"Hey, now!" came a deep, scratchy voice. "Who be hiding there in the hold?"

Kaylie and Hopper froze.

"Come now," the voice commanded. "I know ye be more than rats in there."

Kaylie peeked over the top of one of the crates and saw the skeletal inner frame of the ship's hold. It was jam packed with nets and crates and barrels. And up ahead, near a thick pole that went from ceiling to floor, stood a horrifying man. He wore a gray bandana and a blue coat. Half of his face seemed melted, and the eye on that side was misshapen, pink where the whites should have been, and blood red in the pupil. The man had pistols strung across his chest, and in his right hand he had a jagged notched sword.

Red Eye! His name shot into her thoughts, along with a host of perilous deeds that went with it.

"Out with ye!" the man shouted.

Kaylie and Hopper ducked down. Kaylie tried to shoo away the rat. "Scat!" she whispered. "Go away!"

"I'll not be going away!" the man cried out.

"No, not you," Kaylie said. "I mean, it would be nice if…well, if you went away—"

"Get out here this instant!" the man croaked. "You'll be sorry if'n you don't."

Kaylie heard the man's footsteps getting closer. At the same time, she heard the rat squeaking and nosing around. She also heard Hopper whispering but, because of the rat, she couldn't focus on what he was saying. She kicked with her feet and slapped with her hands and instinctively tried once more to call up her Dreamtreading will. But it did no good. There was still no power there. Not even the slightest trickle.

The rat, meanwhile, had somehow managed to clamber up onto her shoulder and now was making its scratchity, scuttling way toward her neck. It was too much for Kaylie. She shrieked and leaped up.

"Now, I've got ye!" the man growled. There was a metallic flash and a swift whistling sound. And then, there was blood.

CHAPTER THREE

STORIES AND STOWAWAYS

Once a notorious pirate known as "The Sea Wolf," and now a commissioned pirate hunter, Declan Ross had faced his share of difficult spots. He'd escaped a volcanic island in the midst of its cataclysmic eruption. He'd escaped the maelstroms of vicious storms at sea. He'd faced down murderous pirate legends like Thierry Chevillard, Bartholomew Thorne, and the devious miscreant known only as The Merchant. But he'd never felt so cornered as he did when his daughter Anne was involved. And this particular situation had no easy way out. No way out at all.

"What...do...you...mean, the wedding's off?" With each word, Anne's fury grew. "Da...what do you mean?"

"I'm sorry, Anne," Declan Ross replied. "And to you also, Cat. But there's nothing else to be done. Though, truthfully, I should say, the wedding must be postponed...not cancelled."

"But, Da...you promised," Anne said, the simmer gone out of her voice.

"Why, Captain?" Cat asked. "What is so important that it cannot wait until later this afternoon?"

Ross looked to Stede who simply shook his head and shrugged. *Always helpful, that Stede.* "We've just had a visit from Musketoon

MacCready," Ross ventured on. "Anne, you saw him coming. I said he was harmless, but he brought news. Terrible news."

"What, Da?" She gave the door to Cat's cabin a swift kick. It crashed and bounced back, but Stede kept its rebound from hitting anyone. Anne's voice became brittle. "Just tell me."

"The priest who was to marry you," Ross explained, "Father Carroll. His monastery on the south side of Santa Isabel was attacked by a local pirate named Tobias Dredd."

"Tobias Dredd?" Cat spluttered. "He's no local pirate. He's a devil. A legend. They call him Toby Scratch and…the Blood Rose."

"Aye, that's him," Ross explained, "but I'm surprised you've heard so much about him. Dredd has kept clear of the Caribbean for years, but he's been a scourge to the South Pacific. He came to Santa Isabel for Father Carroll, but by God's grace, the priest escaped. Tobias Dredd is in pursuit. He must be stopped."

"Wait," Anne hissed. She was quiet for a few moments. "We weren't here at Santa Isabel Island, the very same place that Captain Dredd happens to be, by coincidence, were we?"

"No," Ross replied quietly.

"That's why you brought us here for the wedding," Anne pressed on. "You insisted we come to the South Pacific. You said it would be secluded, safer than the Caribbean, and an ideal place for our honeymoon."

"That's right," Ross replied, averting his eyes.

"I told you, mon," Stede muttered, shaking his head. "I told you t'be up front wid'da girl."

"Please understand," Ross said. "I did not mean to deceive. Father Brun of the Brethren implored me to say nothing of this mission unless in dire need."

Cat's eyes widened with amazement. He thought about his time with the monks of St. Celestine. They were a special warrior priesthood, dedicated to protecting the most precious relics and resources of God. "The Brethren are in on this?"

Ross nodded. "Not just in on it, as you say, but intimately concerned."

"If Father Brun wanted this kept secret, I understand," Cat said. "They are a close lot, and for good reason. Still, to bring us here without saying anything?"

"Honestly," Ross replied, "I hoped I wouldn't have to trouble you with this at all. I thought you'd be married and off on your honeymoon by the time we got around to Tobias Dredd, but he has rather...forced the issue."

Anne growled out a mouthful of heated air. "I mean no disrespect to Father Carroll," she said, "but he's just a local priest, right? We could get someone else to marry us. A quick set of vows and all, no ceremony. We'll forego the honeymoon for now, so we can race away after Father Carroll."

"I'm afraid not," Ross replied.

"Oh," said Stede, "here it comes, now, mon."

Ross glared at his friend. "Father Carroll is not some random priest," he said quietly. "He is the leader of the South American branch of The Brethren. He's also the caretaker of the Broken Spyglass."

Anne was so angry she did a little hop. "Bro—Broken Spyglass?" she spluttered. "You've got to be joking. Wait, I get it now. This *is* a joke. It's a surprise of some kind, and you're all in on it."

Cat took her by the hand. "I don't think your father would joke about Tobias Dredd. That would be sort of like laughing at a funeral."

"This is no jest, daughter," Ross said. "And we've no time to explain further. No time to waste. If Tobias Dredd gets to Father Carroll first, we'll all regret it." He turned to his quartermaster. "Mr. Stede, chart a course for Lakeba Island."

"Right, mon," Stede said, racing away.

"Lakeba?" Cat said. "I've never heard of it."

"Part of the Fijian Island chain," Ross explained. "That's where Father Carroll will go. I'm sure of it." With that, Captain Ross was gone.

Anne stood very still in the center of Cat's cabin. She blinked slowly and said, "But our wedding…"

Cat took her in his arms. "Our wedding will happen," he said. "I promise. This is merely a brief interruption."

She nodded but couldn't stop thinking, *What if it's not? If Dredd is the demon he seems to be, one of us might be killed, and then, there'd be no wedding…at all.*

* * * * * * *

"Ewww! You killed it!" Kaylie cried out, looking down at the remains of the rat. She slapped Red Eye's hand. "Shame on you."

"B—what?" he grumbled. "The shame's on you, ye blasted stowaways!"

"Stowaways?" Kaylie echoed. "But I—"

Red Eye grabbed Hopper and yanked him to his feet.

"Let him go!" Kaylie shouted.

"Nay, little rat-girl," the man replied. "That I won't do, unless the captain wills it."

Rat-girl? Kaylie thought. *He'd better not call me that again.* But then, she remembered her Dreamtreading will was gone. There was nothing she could do to help Hopper now.

"Come with old Red Eye," he ordered, dragging Hopper away toward a shaft of light in the far corner of the deck.

Hopper stumbled and skinned his knee. "Red Eye!" Hopper exclaimed as he rubbed his knee. "It's me, Hopper! Don't you recognize me?"

"Hopper?" Red Eye let go of the lad and stepped back a few paces. He stared at the boy. So did Kaylie. In the lantern light, she saw that he was completely bald. So odd for a boy his age, but she remembered from the books the tragic circumstances that led to his hair falling out. He had thin eyebrows now, a contented mantle resting above blue eyes that sparkled like huge sapphires.

Red Eye snorted. "Why you be Nathaniel Hopper! I thought you was Brandon Blake and Dolphin's boy now. What ye' be doin' skulking about in the hold a' the *Bruce*?"

Hopper stood up and seemed to stand with rigid military pride. "I am a Blake now, Guv'nor. I'm a mate on his new ship o' the line, the *HMS Canterbury*!"

"But ye didn't answer me question. Ye know yer welcome aboard the *Robert Bruce*, now. No need to stowaway."

Hopper's tanned cheeks deeply reddened. "I wasn't stowing away, Guv'nor...not exactly. I'd come aboard when we were in St. Lucia port, but Cap'n Ross was busy, so I came down here and...uh, fell asleep. Seemed like every time I went to tell him, he was busy, so I just kept to meself."

"Oh, lad," Red Eye exclaimed. "Yer gonna give your new parents a heart attack. Wait'll the captain hears all this. Nathaniel Hopper back on board *The Bruce*, heh, heh. But who's this kinda squeamish rat girl over here? Lands! Look at that red hair. Why she could be Anne's little sister."

"I'm not a rat girl!" Kaylie exclaimed, clambering around and over the crates and barrels. "And, I'm Archer's little sister, not Anne's. I'm Kaylie Keaton. Hopper and I are friends."

Hopper blinked amiably. "Awww," he said. "We are? Wait, why yes, we are."

Red Eye rolled his good eye. "I'm sure ye have a good story 'bout bein' here too. Spare me the details and tell it to the captain. C'mon, the both of ye."

Hopper went up the ladder, followed by Red Eye. Kaylie jogged along behind him and climbed up. A few decks later, Kaylie found herself on the wide main deck of a huge sailing ship. The bright sun on the pure white sails was almost blinding. She held her hand up to shield her eyes.

Sailors were everywhere. Some rolled barrels across the deck. Others climbed like spiders on nets of rope twenty or thirty feet up the ship's three masts. Everyone seemed urgently busy. There was a palpable tension, as if danger could thicken the air and add sizzle to the sun beating down.

Kaylie didn't have much time to stare because Red Eye gave her a little push. They climbed another ladder, turned a corner, and found another man standing by the ship's wheel. His back was turned, but Kaylie thought he looked a little like one of the Three Musketeers.

He wore a long green coat and a wide green hat with a slender white feather sticking out of it. Long curls of sun bleached red hair fell around his collar and mingled with his ragged coppery mustache and beard. His eyes were hazel and locked fiercely onto something straight ahead.

"Lookee what I found, Captain," Red Eye said.

The man at the wheel spun to face them. His coat whirled around him like a cape. He briefly removed his hat and bowed as if Kaylie and Hopper were honored guests, not stowaways.

"Captain Declan Ross, at yer service," he said.

There was a twinkle in his eyes, but Kaylie couldn't tell if it was kindness or mischief. She stood transfixed, blinking stupidly. There he was: Declan Ross, *The Sea Wolf*. He looked exactly like she pictured him, only better.

"I...I'm Kaylie," she mumbled.

"Good to make your acquaintance, Kaylie," Ross said. He smiled wistfully and was still for a moment as if fondly remembering something from long ago. Then, he turned to Hopper. "And, stars alive! If it isn't Nathaniel Hopper Blake." The lad nodded, but the captain said, "By my word there must be quite a story behind all this, but I'm afraid we've no time for it. Not now."

Red Eye said, "What's goin' on, then? I ducked down in the hold t'get a crate for Anne. I come up and we're setting sail? Did I miss the wedding?"

The captain went back to the ship's wheel. "No wedding, not yet," he said. "We've a pirate to catch."

Red Eye hissed, a strangely happy sound, and rattled his cutlass sword in its sheath. "Ah, now, this day keeps gettin' better. Who's it gonna be, then? That rascal, Bellamy? Or no, wait, Edward Teach, I bet. Is it?"

Ross shook his head. "I wish it were," he said. "But not yet. It's Tobias Dredd for us this time."

Red Eye seemed to rock on his heels. He stepped backward a pace. "Dredd?" he gasped. His hand went to the scarred side of his face, fingers probing for his red eye. "We'll not let him get away this time, Captain?"

"No," Ross replied. "We will not. And once we've got him, you can slap the manacles on him yourself and tighten them as you wish."

"Aye, sir!" Red Eye exclaimed. He spun on his heel and raced away to duty. But, as he charged off, he bumped Kaylie. Her left hand unclenched, and a very small roll of yellowed parchment paper fell to the deck.

"What's that, then?" Ross asked.

Kaylie looked down at the little scroll. "I...I don't know what that is."

Hopper bent down and picked up the parchment. "It was in your hand, Miss," he said, holding it out to Kaylie.

"But…I didn't have this before." Kaylie reached out for the scroll, but Captain Ross snatched it away first.

"You'll forgive me, Miss Kaylie," he said. "But I don't know you, and I don't like surprises on my ship." Captain Ross read the parchment to himself. His eyebrows seemed to bristle. His knuckles whitened, and his hands shook. He looked to Hopper and then, to Kaylie. Then, back to the scroll, he read aloud,

"To pirate's bane, a starlit isle,

Upon the seas, you'll face a trial.

To escape your fate, find this token:

The spyglass rare, the spyglass broken."

"What…what does that mean?" Hopper asked.

"What it means, Mr. Hopper," Declan Ross replied, "is that Kaylie has some serious explaining to do."

CHAPTER FOUR

SHARK ATTACK

"Starlit Isle?" Captain Ross muttered to himself. The hazel fire in his eyes smoldered but seemed distant as if kindled in memory. "Miss Kaylie, this rhyme you *happen* to have in your possession was written a very long time ago by one of the first members of the Brethren. His name was Brother Grimwarden. Does that name have any meaning to you?"

Kaylie shifted on her feet. How to answer such a question! Of course, she'd heard that name before, but definitely not in the same context. "It sounds…somewhat familiar," she said hesitantly. "I…I'm not certain."

"Uh, huh," Ross replied, his eyes narrowing. "This rhyme has been passed down from generation-to-generation but only among the Brethren. Father Brun shared it with me, or I'd have never recognized it. So I'm wondering how a young girl came by it and…how that very same young girl ended up appearing quite mysteriously on my ship."

"I know, I know!" Hopper piped. "Why, you've said it yourself, Guv'nor: God works in mysterious ways."

"That He does," Ross said, his wiry mustache barely concealing a wry smile.

"What be the delay, mon?" Stede called up from the deck. A moment later, the muscular quartermaster clambered up and joined the already crowded bridge. "I thought we be headin' right off."

"So we are," Ross replied. "You've charted the course to Lakeba?"

"Of course, mon," Stede said. "We b'havin' rare good luck. There be prevailin' winds dis time of year, the whole way, most."

Declan Ross slammed a fist into his palm. "It's a race to Lakeba, then," he said. "Dredd's *Red Corsair* is fast, but I imagine Father Carroll has something smaller and faster. And *The Bruce* is faster still. We might just get there first. Stede, all speed."

"Yeah, mon!" Stede cried, bouncing from the quarterdeck down to the main deck and shouting orders as he ran.

"What'll I do with these two?" Red Eye asked.

"Red Eye, you'll do nothing with them," Ross replied. "See to our cannons. When we run across Toby Scratch, I want *The Bruce* ready to unload any and all guns at my command."

"That'll be my pleasure, Sir," Red Eye muttered lustily. He too vanished from the quarterdeck.

Ross turned to his young guests. "Mister Hopper," he said, "I wonder if perhaps you could teach Miss Kaylie a few of the needed chores on *The Bruce*. A good day's work, cleaning the poop deck, might jog her memory a bit. Specifically, I wish to know how and why you came aboard *The Bruce* and how you came by the Rhyme of the Spyglass Broken."

"Jog my memory?" Kaylie replied. "I've studied the field of neuroscience for some time, and I'm reasonably certain that memory doesn't work like that."

Ross blinked repeatedly, and his mouth fell open. "What?"

Kaylie sighed. "While it is true that the hippocampus and the frontal cortex of the brain work together to analyze sensory input, I highly doubt that some menial task or chore on the *poop deck* will help me access the correct neural networks required."

"Captain Ross?" Hopper asked. "What language is Kaylie speaking?"

"I'm quite sure I don't know," Ross said. "What I do know is that there is much more to Miss Kaylie than meets the eye. Now then, off with the lot of you. I have winds to catch."

"C'mon, then, Kaylie," Hopper said, taking her by the hand. "We've work to do."

Kaylie liked the way Hopper took her hand. There was something sweet and very gentlemanly about it. And, somehow, she felt she'd known him for a lot longer than she really had.

"What's going on?" Hopper asked in a whisper as they crossed the main deck to the portside. "Where did you get the note?"

"I…I don't know," said Kaylie. "It was just there in my hand."

"That…seems, erhm, odd."

"It's no odder than this clothing I'm wearing," she said.

Hopper stopped their progress. "What's odd about your clothes?" he asked curiously. "You're dressed like any ship's mate would be, dressed for the hot sun, I'd say."

"I know," Kaylie replied. "It's just that I wasn't wearing all this before. I had my regular…uh…clothes on…uh…before."

"Before what?" Hopper asked.

Kaylie swallowed audibly. "Before, uh, I came aboard the ship."

"What were you wearing then?"

And I thought I was curious, Kaylie thought. "Nevermind. It's just different."

She and Hopper stumbled sideways and steadied themselves on the port rail. The ship had lurched and caught them both off guard. Choruses of shouting rang out on the deck. There came a series of deep flapping sounds, and Kaylie watched as each of *The Bruce's* massive trapezoidal sails seemingly grabbed great bellies of wind. The ship lunged forward and hummed with motion.

"This ship's fast," Kaylie muttered.

"Few faster," Hopper said. "You'll get used to it. C'mon then, poop deck's waiting."

In spite of Kaylie's fears, the poop deck turned out to be a high deck platform in the very back of the ship. It had a horseshoe-shaped railing, several locked chests, and a dozen or more rings of metal where ropes had been tied off.

Hopper grabbed a bucket of soapy water and two scrub brushes. "Captain Ross will want it sparkling clean by six bells," he said. "If not, he'll be throwing ye to the sharks."

"He wouldn't!" Kaylie exclaimed.

"Of course he wouldn't," Hopper explained. "He's not a pirate anymore."

"Are there sharks out there?" she asked.

"See for ye'self," Hopper said, pointing a scrub brush over the rail.

Kaylie drew close and bent over the rail. Down below, large black fins cut through the turbulent, dark green water. Just then, a huge shark blasted up out of the water. It rose impossibly high into the air, coming straight towards the kids at the rail. It snapped its teeth. Hopper and Kaylie fell backward onto the deck.

"Ye see," Hopper said, "the sharks be hungry."

"If it's okay with you," Kaylie said, "I'm going to work over here…away from the rail."

Hopper laughed. "Me too."

Hopper and Kaylie set to work. They sloshed water onto the deck and scrubbed hard at the wood. The wood was filthy and smelled like dead fish. Dried mud and sand had been ground into the cracks between the boards.

"Do you know anything about Captain Dredd?" asked Kaylie.

"No," Hopper said. "I've never heard of him. But, if he makes Declan Ross nervous, that's more than enough cause to scare the likes of me."

They said little more to each other and, for several hours, they worked steadily. The sun burned hot, and their muscles ached. Kaylie stood up a moment to stretch her back.

"Hopper, look," she said, pointing over the stern rail. "There's another ship out there."

Hopper stood. "Where?" he asked. "The sun's too bright. I don't see—"

He never finished the sentence. In The Robert Bruce's wake, materializing out of the sun's glare on the water, a dark ship appeared. It had three sharp gray sails that reminded Hopper of the shark's fins.

The other ship began to come about. Hopper saw a black flag. It flapped in the wind at the top of the middle mast. A stark white skull grinned from the black flag, and maybe crossed bones behind it, but Hopper couldn't distinguish the details of the design. Still, it was enough to know: "Pirates," Hopper whispered. Then, as the chasing ship turned more, he saw a row of black holes along the ship's side.

"Are those what I think they are?" Kaylie asked.

"Cannons!" Hopper shouted. "It looks like they're aiming at us!"

Hopper raced across the poop deck to the stair. "Captain!" he yelled with Kaylie racing after. "Captain Ross, there's a ship out there! There are pirates out there!"

"What's dat you say?" Stede replied. He looked up from the wheel as Kaylie and Hopper descended to the quarterdeck.

"Behind us!" Kaylie cried.

"Mister Stede, Guv'nor," Hopper said, "a ship's in our wake and gaining, a pirate ship with many guns. Training on us now, I think!"

"Wot, no!" Stede growled. "Port or starboard cannon?"

Hopper hesitated. "I...I'm not sure. Coming out of the sun."

"Starboard!" Kaylie exclaimed. "The ship was swinging to his left, and that's port. So it would be the ship's starboard cannons."

"Dat be good!" Stede muttered, flexing his massive shoulders, yanking the wheel to turn the ship hard to starboard. "Go find Captain Ross!"

"C'mon, Kaylie!" Hopper yelled, nearly yanking her down the quarterdeck steps. He and Kaylie climbed down and sprinted across the deck. Hopper rounded the main mast, tripped over a rope, and crashed at Captain Ross's feet.

Kaylie lunged but hooked a foot on the same line. She banged her chin smartly on the deck, but lurched quickly to her knees. "Captain!"

"Here, now," Captain Ross replied. "Looking for more work already?"

"There's a pirate out there, Captain!" Kaylie shouted.

"What?" the captain shouted. "Nonsense! My man Nock up in the crow's nest would have—"

"It had gray sails," Hopper explained. "Looked like shark fins!"

"Shark fins?" the captain repeated. "Here? It can't be!"

Suddenly, there were three muffled booms. The chasing ship had fired its cannons.

CHAPTER FIVE

TURNING THE TABLES

A cannonball tore through the sail over their heads, bursting through like a dark fist. Another cannonball hit the water next to *The Bruce's* port bow. And with a loud *FOOM*, water sprayed twenty feet into the air.

"Get down!" Captain Ross yelled.

Kaylie and Hopper, who had just gotten back to his feet, hit the deck hard.

But the captain didn't get down. He sprinted toward the rear of the ship and shouted as he went. "Red Eye!" the captain yelled, " as soon as we've come about, fire the starboard cannons!"

Red Eye didn't answer, but *The Bruce's* cannons did. The booms sounded like fireworks, ten blasts in a row. They were so loud that Kaylie had to cover her ears.

"Did we get him?" Hopper asked, leaping to his feet.

Kaylie crawled to the rail, stood, and looked up. "I can't see. Too much smoke."

"C'mon!" Hopper beckoned, and they raced after Captain Ross until they met upon the quartedeck.

"That you, Stede!" Captain Ross exclaimed. "Brilliant maneuver. You've saved us again, but if you don't mind…"

Stede nodded graciously and stepped back from the wheel. "D'blasted smoke, mon," he said. "I can't tell if we got d'mon."

"Again, Red Eye!" Captain Ross yelled, continuing to turn the wheel. "Once more with the starboard long guns!"

CRACK! A cannonball crashed through the rail behind Captain Ross. Shards of broken wood flew all over the deck. Bits and pieces remained snarled in his wild coppery hair. "Too close!" the captain yelled. Ross looked up at the sails and spun the wheel.

"He's goin' fer the masts!" Stede growled.

"That'll never do," Ross muttered. "Especially not now. I need more sail, Stede! We need more distance between us, at our long guns limit, but too much range for him!"

"I'm on it!" Stede cried out, leaping from the quarterdeck and sprinting away.

"God bless that man!" Ross said, a fiery gleam in his eye.

There came more faraway booms, sounds like a thunderstorm raging on the horizon, and huge fountains of water sprayed up, port and starboard.

"Fool!" Captain Ross yelled. "Don't you know, you never threaten a wolf! Ha, ha! Stede's done it. He's trimmed the sails! Just a little more and then, watch out!"

The Robert Bruce lurched again and, to Kaylie, it felt as if the ship were so agile that it rode not upon the waves, but on the clouds. She felt the momentum shift in her stomach, like riding a sideways elevator. Wind buffeted her hair, back, arms, and lower legs. The water slapped the hull so rapidly it sounded like machine gun fire.

"The long guns, now, Red Eye!" Ross cried out. "All, fire!"

Kaylie and Hopper rose up to look. But the sound of twenty thunderclaps made them drop back to the deck. *The Robert Bruce* seemed to rock hard to port.

Then, it was strangely quiet for a few moments. "What's happening?" Hopper whispered.

"I don't know," Kaylie whispered back.

"Ha, ha!" Captain Ross roared. "We got'im this time! Look there, my fine stowaways, look there!"

Kaylie and Hopper wobbled to their feet. Through the clouds of smoke, they saw that the dark ship was on fire. And where the pirate flag was, a huge white flag now flew.

"Ha, ha!" Captain Ross shouted. "The Great White Pirate is flyin' a white flag of surrender!"

"Great White Pirate?" Kaylie asked.

"Captain Strylun Petrov, actually," Captain Ross explained. "He's a Russian pirate who has the nerve to call himself a great white shark. Like a shark, Petrov always surprise attacks his targets, cripples them before they know what's hit them. But, not this time. You gave us warning, saved us for sure."

"You mean it's not Captain Dredd?" Kaylie asked.

"Dredd?" Ross barked. "Oh, no. With Dredd, we'd not have fared so well, not so easily, at least."

Captain Ross put *The Robert Bruce* on course to close on the burning ship. In moments, they pulled up alongside the smoking vessel. Kaylie and Hopper watched as Captain Ross's crew fished pirates out of the water.

"Take 'em to the brig!" Captain Ross commanded.

Kaylie counted fifteen pirates, including a man with a black captain's hat. He was tall and broad. Sopping wet, dark blond hair leaked out from beneath his hat. His furious eyes burned beneath a shelf-like heavy brow, and a raw scar sluiced up from his jaw line.

"He doesn't look too happy," Hopper whispered. "And no mistake."

Kaylie strained to see better. "Is that all there is? I mean, aren't there any more men?"

"Nay, lass," Captain Ross said. "The rest didn't survive."

"Look!" Hopper yelled. He pointed over the rail.

They all turned. The burning ship was sinking. In moments, it disappeared beneath the water with a hiss.

CHAPTER SIX

QUESTIONS

Captain Ross raised a glass and tapped it with a spoon.

What is that about? Kaylie wondered.

"Quiet, ye louts!" Captain Ross shouted.

The sailors at the dining table went quiet. Kaylie and Hopper sat on the captain's left; Stede and Red Eye on the right. They were in a large room at the back of the ship, the captain's cabin. Hanging lanterns lit the room in orange, gold, and red, and reflected back from the deck-to-ceiling rows of square windows that looked out on the invisible night sea.

Captain Ross turned and announced to the group, "I give you, Kaylie and Hopper, the heroes of the day!"

All the other sailors raised their glasses and shouted, "Hear, hear!"

"Now, be seated," the captain said, "and let's eat!"

"Aren't we going to pray?" came a question from the back of the room. The accent was heavily Spanish.

Kaylie ducked left and right, trying to get a clear view of the speaker. She couldn't be sure, but she thought it was the dark, weather-beaten man sitting closest to the windows. He wasn't just weather-beaten. His skin was dark with tan, scarred and cracked so severely that he almost appeared to have scales. That's when she saw it. Cradled in the man's massive arms was a three-foot alligator. It looked a little different from the gators Kaylie had seen. Its head and jaws were more narrow and tapered, and it had thick stripes of mustard yellow and muted green. She thought it might be stuffed, but then, its yellow eyes blinked.

Kaylie squeaked, "There's an alligator at the end of the table!"

"Yes," Captain Ross said, slurping a spoon of stew. "His name is Caiman, and he has a gator in his lap, too."

A general chuckle rumbled at the head of the table.

"I said, aren't we going to pray?" the man called Caiman asked. "Especialmente since we have been blessed with so great a victory this day."

Captain Ross's spoon was already half in his mouth. A bit of stew dribbled onto his beard. "Of course," the captain said, putting down his spoon. "I am duly corrected. Please, Caiman, if you would."

The gator in Caiman's lap hissed, but he tapped it on its nose. It closed its mouth, and Caiman closed his eyes. "Gracias, Almighty God, for keeping us safe today. This victory was yours, and glory to your name. May you continue to bless us with powerful winds and guide us to our destination. We are grateful for this food. We pray…en el nombre del Padre, el Hijo, y el Santo Espiritu, amen."

"Amen," Kaylie murmured. She'd never heard a prayer like that before. She marveled at the strange man with the gator in his lap.

"Thank you, Caiman," Captain Ross said, diving back into his stew.

The cabin filled with clinks, clanks, and slurps. There was a tap on Kaylie's shoulder, and Hopper whispered, "I think the captain has decided you are trustworthy."

"I hope so," Kaylie said. "I really don't know where the scrap with the rhyme came from. I don't like when people doubt me."

"After today, the captain at least must know whose side you're on." Hopper nodded and went back to his stew.

Kaylie thoughtfully worked on her own bowl. The stew was savory, full of potatoes, carrots, onions, all swimming in brown gravy. There were also chunks of chewy white meat. It wasn't chicken, but Kaylie was afraid to ask about it. Besides, she had other questions burning on her mind.

She leaned over to Hopper again. "Where are we going, now?" she asked. "Captain Ross seemed so urgent to get somewhere fast, but now, we're just sitting around down here."

"We're moving as fast as the wind will take us," said a young man to Kaylie's left. His hair was blonde and unruly, his face was tan, and his eyes were so blue that Kaylie had to blink and look away. He spoke again, "And while we are just 'sitting around down here,' another group of men are taking their turn manning the operation of *The Robert Bruce*."

"Oh," Kaylie said.

The young man extended his hand. "I'm Cat," he said as they shook. "My given name is Griffin, but everyone calls me Cat."

"Oh!" Kaylie said, much too loud for her own comfort. "I mean, it's nice to meet you, Cat."

Cat leaned back and gestured. "And this radiant vision to my left is my future wife, Anne."

"Radiant vision," Anne scoffed. "Oh, please. Cut the bloated words. I've already consented to be your wife." Her words were terse, but she smiled as she spoke. She reached out across Cat to shake Kaylie's hand. "Welcome aboard *The Robert Bruce*," she said. "It'll be nice to have some female company. Much more interesting conversation."

"Hey!" Cat feigned offense and laughed. "She's most assuredly correct."

Kaylie giggled, but she couldn't stop staring at Anne. *She could be a Keaton,* she thought. *All that flowing red hair. So pretty.*

They ate in silence until Captain Ross pushed his bowl away. It made such a grating sound that everyone turned to stare at the captain.

But Ross had fixed his eyes on a man on the other side of the table, seated next to Caiman. This man had pale blond hair, pulled back into a tail. He was narrow of face and build, and sat extremely straight in his chair. He had restless pale blue eyes that seemed to look everywhere in the cabin but to Captain Ross.

"Nock!" the Captain called out. "If it weren't for Kaylie and Hopper, that shark of a pirate, Petrov, might'a sunk us. Why didn't you warn us?"

"It was an inexcusable error, Captain," Nock replied. His voice was melodious, light, and velvety, but there was an echo of sorrow to his words. "Petrov sailed at us right out of the sun. I did not see him until he was upon us."

Captain Ross frowned. "Not inexcusable," he said. "But an error still. From now on, when the teeth of the sun blinds you from a certain position, I'll want you to be more or less a spider up there in the rigging. Clamber about until you can find less compromised vantage points."

"Yes, sir," Nock replied, a bloom of crimson rising in his cheeks. "We will not be caught unaware again."

Ross threw a hasty nod at Nock and said, "Now then, my guests, it grows late. You best be off to bed. Red Eye here will see you to yer hammocks."

"Do we have to go to bed now?" Hopper asked.

"Scrubbin' a deck's hard work," Red Eye said. "Ain't ye tired?"

"A little," Kaylie said. "But before we sleep, could you tell us what you're going to do with us?"

"Do with you?" Captain Ross said with raised eyebrows. He glanced at Red Eye. "You still be thinkin' you're some sort of prisoners?"

"My father wouldn't dare harm you," Anne said. "Would you, Da?"

He shook his head. "Not even if you were, in fact, stowaways," he said. "Or worse. Not at your young age. Too much promise, too much time to change."

"But I wonder," Captain Ross said, "If maybe ye could help us on our mission."

"The mission to catch Captain Tobias Dredd?" Hopper asked.

Captain Ross snorted in surprise. "Now, how on earth did ye know that?"

"You told us," Kaylie explained. "Up by the ship's steering wheel thingy."

"Thingy," Cat chuckled, taking a sip from a wooden cup. "First time I've heard it called that."

"It was when I first brought them up from the hold," Red Eye said. "You said the wedding was off uh, fer now, 'cause we be needin' t'get after Dredd."

"Ah, so I did," Ross replied thoughtfully. "So much gets muddled when twenty-four pound cannonballs are sailing 'round yer head."

"So is that it?" Kaylie asked. "We're trying to catch Captain Dredd?"

"Not going to catch him," Red Eye muttered, a distinct edge to his voice.

Captain Ross glanced sideways at Red Eye and said, "Actually, our main goal is to find a priest named Father Andrew Carroll before Dredd does."

"Why?" Kaylie asked.

"Because Dredd wants to capture him," Ross said. "He carries a very particular relic of great value."

"The broken spyglass?" Kaylie asked.

Ross nodded. "Father Carroll has it in his possession," he said. "Or so it is believed. That is why Dredd went after him on Santa Isabel. That is why we must get to Carroll first."

"Not the only reason," Cat said jovially, hugging Anne close to him. "Father Carroll needs to perform our wedding."

"You're getting married?" Kaylie squeaked. "I knew it!"

"What?" Cat looked at her blankly.

Kaylie gave herself a mental facepalm. "What I mean is, you looked so much in love…I just knew that you were engaged."

Captain Ross cleared his throat and looked away. "Anne and Cat, again, I cannot express enough how sorry I am to delay your most blessed day. But Tobias Dredd is a dangerous pirate, even the grandson of Black Bart himself. We've chased him half way around this world, and he has eluded us. Now, we're racing him to an island called Lakeba. It's one of the islands of Fiji."

"Is Father Carroll on the island?" Hopper asked.

"I cannot be certain, lad," said Captain Ross. "But I suspect if Carroll wanted to hide anywhere, it would be Lakeba. He began his clergy career as a missionary there, trying to reach the native people of Lakeba for God."

"See now, Guv'nor," Hopper said, "that's just what I don't get. I mean, this Dredd is a hard man, a killer, right? What does he want with a priest and some old broken spyglass? Not goin' to confession, I imagine."

"Not likely," Red Eye groused.

"Mister Hopper," Ross said, "You've a keen mind." But the captain did not answer Hopper's questions. Instead, he rapped once more with his spoon on the glass, stood and announced, "What do you rogues think this is, a holiday? Get back to your stations! There are tired men who need your relief. Off with you!"   ·

A storm of grumbling later, the captain's cabin cleared out. Along with Kaylie and Hopper, Cat and Anne remained. Red Eye lingered near the door and said, "Captain, I ain't asked ye fer much since I been aboard."

Ross stirred uncomfortably and turned. "No, you haven't," he said. "You've served me, *The Robert Bruce*, and our crew with uncommon bravery and loyalty. Say what's on your mind."

"It's just this, sir," Red Eye said, worrying at a line of scars on his face. "I'm asking now, asking that ye keep yer promise...about Captain Dredd."

Ross nodded thoughtfully. "I haven't forgotten my promise, Bill," he said. "I will keep it."

When Red Eye had gone, Captain Ross closed his cabin door and took his seat. He turned back to his audience of four and said, "Some of the details we're about to discuss should not be overheard by all."

"Why, Da?" Anne asked.

"Because some of our deck hands are unproven," he said. "I don't know rightly if I can trust them."

Kaylie found a spot on the table to stare at. "Former pirates," she whispered.

"That's right," Ross said, "and some...not so former, I suspect. Anne and Cat, I am assigning Miss Kaylie and Master Hopper to your care. With all due respect to these younger ones, I cannot allow information like this to travel. What I reveal to you now is for your ears alone."

"Yes, Da," Anne replied.

"And, Miss Kaylie," Ross went on, "I wouldn't share this information with you at all if not for your actions this afternoon. That, and the fact that you seem to already be entwined with the fate of the broken spyglass. Do not make me regret my trust in you."

Kaylie felt as if she'd been clamped in a vice. "I...I won't, sir," she whispered.

"Now then, Tobias Dredd wants Father Carroll with a murderous passion because he may be the only Englishman alive who knows how to use the broken spyglass to find the Isle of Stars."

"The starlight isle," Hopper said. "From the note?"

"Yes," said the captain, "from the note. Legend says this island holds a treasure worth three times the whole world. Jewels beyond count, precious and rare, some that possess their own light. It's said that, when the jewels are set alight at night, it makes the island vanish, cloaked by the star strewn-sky."

"Just like the stars on the open sea?" Hopper asked.

"Aye, lad," said the captain. "At night, the jewels look like stars. Ye could be staring right at the island and not even know it was there."

"But why wouldn't you just look for the island during the day?" Kaylie asked.

"You could," Captain Ross replied. "Many have made the attempt to no avail. My friends in The Brethren say there is a whirling sea of mists that curls around the small island during the day. Ye could send a fleet a'ships into that mist. They'd either crash into each other or come out all over the Pacific. But they wouldn't find the Isle of Stars. But once, by sheer accident, someone did find the island."

"Who?" Cat asked.

"Tobias Dredd," Ross replied. "Of all the cursed luck, Toby Scratch himself crashed right into the Isle of Stars many, many years ago. It was after a harsh mutiny aboard his former ship, but he was bested, beaten to within an inch of his life, and set adrift in an old cutter. Somehow, he drifted through that mist wall, and the cutter got stuck in a crook of rock. When night fell, Dredd saw the jewels shining. But injured and delirious with fever, he couldn't manage to get the cutter into shore. He lost consciousness, and the tide took him back out. When he awoke, old Dredd knew what he'd seen. And for thirty years since, Captain Tobias Dredd has been searching fer the island."

"After the jewels," Kaylie whispered.

"Yes," Captain Ross replied. "If Dredd gets to Father Carroll before we do, he'll force the priest to take him back to the Isle of Stars. Then, he'll kill Father Carroll and strip the island of its jewels."

"But there's more to it, Da," Anne said quietly. "Isn't there?"

Captain Ross didn't reply.

"The Brethren are involved in this," Cat said. "There must be something more to this Isle of Stars than a massive treasure."

"There is," Ross said, "but they haven't told me what. Oh, they've hinted and riddled at it, but I've no clear idea what it's all about."

"What'd they say?" Kaylie asked. "I'm pretty good at riddles."

Ross smiled. "So much like you, Anne, when you were little," he said. "Clever are you, Miss Kaylie? Well, here is what Father Brun of the Brethren told me. 'No black hearted pirate must ever be allowed to come to the Isle of Stars. It is the last of what's left from before.'"

"Before?" Kaylie echoed. "Before what?"

"That's just what I asked. His answer was just as mysterious and only leads to more questions that he would not answer. Father Brun said, 'The Isle of Stars is all that's left of the world before…before it all went bad.'"

CHAPTER SEVEN

LAKEBA ISLAND

"LAND HO!" a clear voice called from one of the masts high above. Kaylie gazed up into the rigging and, sure enough, Nock's slender form appeared, dancing in and out of the glaring sun. He moved with infinitely more grace than a common spider, traversing the netting, ascending and descending the rope lines, and swinging one-handed around masts and cross spars. "Lakeba Island to port!"

Kaylie and Hopper ran to the port rail. It had been a frantic week at sea with Ross pushing the crew of *The Robert Bruce* for every possible extra half-knot of speed. But the winds had been strong and the sea, kind. According to Stede, they'd made the journey from Santa Isabel to the isle of Lakeba as fast as might be hoped.

Kaylie gazed out upon a green island. So many variations of green! Pine, emerald, olive, moss, jade, and more, but among the darkest green thatches, irregular cliffs of white and gray limestone rose up. These startling formations were pocked with toothy black openings, hollows, and caves.

"Do you know what that's called?" Kaylie asked.

Hopper rolled his eyes. "It's an island."

Kaylie looked sideways at her new friend. "I know *that*," she said. "I'm talking about the cliffs there. There's a name for that kind of topography."

Hopper blinked. "B-what?"

"I'm glad you asked," Kaylie said. "It's called karst topography. It's any landscape formed of soluble rock such as limestone, leading to underground drainage and the formation of sinkholes and caves."

Hopper shook his head as if to ward off a mischievous insect. "You are speaking that strange language again." He laughed. Kaylie joined in with a chorus of giggles, but then they both grew silent and stared at the island.

It was beautiful but, at the same time, mysterious and unnerving. Ghostly white clouds drifted around the peaks of its low mountains, vague shadows in the distance suggested a deep, untamed terrain, and black caves stared out from the pale limestone like spider's eyes.

"I wonder, Miss Kaylie," Hopper said, "if we might have picked the wrong journey upon which to stowaway."

Kaylie shivered. "I was thinking the same thing."

* * * * * * *

After a bouncy ride in a ten-seat rowboat called a cutter, Kaylie and Hopper stepped ashore on Lakeba Island. While Captain Ross ordered his sailors to pull the rowboats out of the bright blue water, Kaylie watched the motley assortment of men emerge from the surf.

Stede, *The Bruce's* burly quartermaster, clamped his giant clam-shell hand on the prow of one cutter and dragged it ashore all by himself. Still, Stede was dwarfed by Jules who hadn't even waited for the passengers to get out of the boat he drug ashore. Red Eye, while smaller than many of the others, radiated intensity, charging through the surf with great, loping strides.

And then, there was a very unusual man carrying an armful of small barrels. He wasn't dressed like the others. Dapper in a heavy frock coat over a frilly white shirt, he seemed ready for a courtly ballroom dance, not an island incursion. His wild black hair, shifting, dark eyes, and rapier-thin mustache gave him a sinister look. The way he moved, darting in and out of the other sailors made Kaylie nervous. *What is he up to? And what's in those barrels?*

Even Cat and Anne showed a bit of ferocious zeal, wearing similar roguish grins as they towed their cutter in the low surf.

They may be British Navy, Kaylie thought, *but these people are as tough and terrifying as any pirates I've ever imagined.* And those swords…those wickedly sharp, curving cutlass swords—they glistened like teeth bared in the jaws of some massive beast.

"Come on, keep up!" Red Eye ordered. He waved his cutlass above his head, and it gleamed in the hot sun. "We've a long march ahead!"

Cat and Anne leaped onto the shore. "We've got no time to waste," Cat said, gesturing to Kaylie and Hopper. "Let's go, you louts!"

"They're not prisoners," Anne protested, playfully stepping in front of the startled kids.

"I know it well," Cat replied. "Nonetheless, we need to get moving."

"Ho, ho!" someone shouted in heavily French-accented English. Kaylie spun and saw that it was the suspicious man with the thin mustache and strange little barrels. "To ze' island we go, mon Capitaine!"

"Jacques!" Captain Ross grumbled. "Why did you bring black powder barrels onto the island?"

"What, these little things?" St. Pierre replied. "Ho, ho, they are but petit charges!"

"Yes, yes," Ross replied, "so I see. But the question remains: why did you bring any black powder at all?"

"Facile, mon Capitaine!" St. Pierre lifted an eyebrow mischievously. "Lakeba Isle may pose problems. And…there are no problems in life 'zat cannot be solved by a barrel of black powder…or three."

The Bruce's crew, to a man, rippled with laughter. Even Captain Ross chuckled at St. Pierre's words.

Where have I heard that before? Kaylie wondered. *I know I've heard something like that before.* There was little time to ponder. The crew of *The Bruce* finished securing the cutters, ran up a low hill of sand, and plunged into the thick jungle foliage. Deckhands led the way, their machetes carving a wedge-shaped path into the green. Vines hung down in their path, and the dancing machetes took them out one by one except, Kaylie noticed, one particularly thick green vine. This strange, looping vine had small white markings along its length, a thick bulb of a head, and a flickering pink tongue.

"Ooh, look at that snake!" Kaylie said.

Hopper said, "Don't worry, Kaylie. That snake don't have a diamond shaped head, so it's probably not poisonous."

"Oh, I'm not worried," Kaylie said, reaching up to tickle the underside of the snake's head. "This is a Pacific boa constrictor. Not poisonous, not really very dangerous, unless you're a rodent." Then she giggle-snorted. "Ha, if you were a rodent, Hopper, you'd be a rodent of unusual size. Ha, ha!"

Hopper stared back at her, his blue eyes amiable as always, but blinking with confusion. "I, uh…I 'spect you're right, Miss Kaylie."

Kaylie's inner mirth melted away, for she knew exactly why Hopper hadn't understood the reference. *What have I done?* she thought again, and not for the last time. Once more, she reached for her Dreamtreader will, tried to call up even a tiny surge of creative power, but there was nothing there. Nothing.

Ross and the expedition party from *The Bruce* plodded on for what felt like days but had really been several hours. They took a break for some dried meat sticks and fresh water but then were off again. After picking their way through the tall plants and vines for another hour or more, they stopped. The jungle had become silent.

Kaylie felt sure that danger lurked nearby, but she couldn't see it.

"What's going on?" Hopper asked. "Why did we—"

"Shhh!" Red Eye held his hook up to his lips. "Not another word," he hissed.

They had come to a clearing deep in the Lakeba jungle, but no one moved.

Suddenly, as if he had appeared out of thin air, a muscular dark-skinned native stood in front of them. He wore bead and bone necklaces, pieces bleached bone-white mixed with pieces of other colors, black, dark purple, and red—especially red. Belts of dyed material coiled around his hips, over a green cloth wrap.

But what amazed Kaylie the most was his wild hair. He wore it high and thick with wiry dark patches sticking out this way and that—even his beard. The man's eyes were wild too, and he stared as if angry. He held a vicious-looking spear in his left hand. He raised the spear once and drove it to the ground.

All at once, dozens of natives came out of the trees all around them. They were armed with stone hatchets and spears.

Oh no! Kaylie thought. *We're trapped!*

CHAPTER EIGHT

FATHER CARROLL

Captain Declan Ross did not back away from the natives. "We are looking for Father Carroll," he said. "Do you know where he is?"

The first native said, "I am Chief Timosofertu. Who are you?"

Hopper whispered to Kaylie, "The savage speaks English?"

"He's not a savage," Kaylie grumbled back. "He's a human being."

Hopper's eyes grew huge. "I…I didn't mean—"

"I am Captain Declan Ross," the captain announced, his voice oak-hard and wind-resonant. "I serve the British Royal Navy and have come far to protect Father Carroll."

"Protect him?" the chief asked. "You not—how to say—you not of clan, the man, Dredd?"

Captain Ross shook his head and said, "No, we most certainly are not a part of Dredd's clan. We want to capture Dredd to protect Father Carroll."

"Capture?" Red Eye muttered.

"Stow it," Ross hissed.

He's not convinced, Kaylie thought.

"We see," Chief Timosofertu replied. "True, we see. Come, follow me. And do not touch swords or you feel spears, heh, heh."

After a few minutes walk, they came to a wide clearing, surrounded by high, leaning trees and nearly roofed by dense foliage and loops of hanging vine. Dozens of straw and mud huts formed a close network within, and many dark-skinned natives wandered here and there, seemingly oblivious to the newcomers.

"They all have such wild, tall hair," Hopper whispered. "But the chief's hair is wildest and tallest."

"Maybe it's a sign of authority," Kaylie replied.

"Shhh," Cat urged, leaning close. "I'd rather we didn't offend them. Did you notice the hook weapons they carry?"

Kaylie had noticed. And, she noticed again…and shuddered.

Chief Timosofertu led their party to the largest hut on the other side of the clearing. It was an oblong structure, deeper than the rest too, and seemed to be more supported by timber. Slats of white wood crisscrossed each panel of straw, and purplish-green vines coiled tightly at every junction.

The chief motioned for Ross and Stede to step inside, but spearmen barred the path for the others. Hopper had other ideas. He darted beneath the spears and was inside before anyone could react. Kaylie followed suit and was relieved to hear the spearmen chuckling outside.

The moment she set eyes upon the interior, Kaylie thought, *It's a school!*

In front of a class full of islanders, young and old, stood a white-skinned man. He had wavy dark hair and round glasses. There was a small rectangular board in his hand. And he was writing a few words on it with chalk.

Then the man looked up, saw Captain Ross and Stede, and, with a slight tremor in his hand, he slowly lowered the chalkboard. "If you be pirates," he said, "I have nothing of value here save the word of God. And that I will give to you freely."

"Father Carroll?" Captain Ross asked.

"Yes," the man replied.

All the natives turned to watch the conversation.

The captain said, "I am Captain Declan Ross of His Majesty's Royal Navy. I have come to offer you and your settlement safety."

"Safety?" Carroll asked. "Safety from what?"

"From the pirate Tobias Dredd," Ross replied.

"Not again," Carroll said. "Perhaps I should end today's lesson. Then, we can talk."

The priest said a few words to the natives in their language, "Raica iko ni mitaka."

"I like the sound of their speech," Hopper said. "I wonder what he just told them."

"I wouldn't worry," Kaylie replied. "It was probably just something like: Shish kebob them if they move funny."

The natives got up from their bench seats. As they left the hut, Kaylie noticed they were all smiling. *A day off of school,* she thought. *Even here it's a thrill.*

When the others had gone, only Chief Timosofertu remained. Captain Ross said, "You must be a man of extraordinary seamanship, escaping Dredd so far like you have. But I fear—" Ross's words shut off at a metallic click.

In the hand opposite the small chalkboard, Father Carroll held a bulky, multi-barreled pistol. "Fear," he said, "is the appropriate word, Scoundrel. I don't know how you found me, but be ye aware, I've no disinclination about delivering God's judgment swiftly. This pistol can discharge five shots in less than a minute."

"And you'll not need to discharge a single one of them," Ross said. "For one, we are not scoundrels but friends. And two, there are children present. It would be rather unpleasant to leave such a colorful scene in their young memories."

"Friends?" Carroll echoed. "A scoundrel may speak friend with a forked tongue. What proof have you of more noble intentions?"

"Father Brun has taught you well," Ross said. "But then, of course, the Brethren often do."

"You know of Brun?"

"Brun and Dominguez and many others," Ross went on. "In fact, it is on behalf of Father Brun that I have sailed my ship so far to see to your safety. Well that, and my daughter would kill me if you were not able to perform her wedding ceremony as planned."

"Ross," Father Carroll echoed thoughtfully. "Wait, you mean Griffin Thorne and Anne Ross—that wedding?"

Ross nodded. "They are right outside."

Father Carroll secured the pistol. "Lord, have mercy in such times as these. I am dreadfully sorry about the pistol."

"Think nothing of it," Ross said. "In my line of work, it happens quite often."

"Father Brun is a crafty one," Carroll said. "He has a unique way of gathering people with the right combination of talents. I should have known—with names like Thorne and Ross—that this would be no ordinary wedding."

Stede tapped the captain's shoulder and said, "We ought to be gettin' d'priest t'safety, don't ya think?"

Ross nodded. "My quartermaster is right, Father Carroll. You can't stay here."

"It's as remote a place as I could think of," he said. "How could Dredd find me here?"

"Your monastery back on Santa Isabel. Dredd no doubt took any of the remaining Brethren as captives."

"But they are sworn to secrecy."

Ross exchanged glances with Stede. "They may well be," he said. "But...what is it Christ said to His disciples? 'The spirit is willing, but the flesh is weak'?"

"He would torture them? To find me?"

"He would turn a man inside out to get to you."

"You know why he be seekin' ya' wid such a terrible fire, don't ya', mon?" Stede asked.

"Of course," said Carroll. "The treasure of Starlight Isle."

"Do you know where it is?" Hopper blurted out.

"And who is this young fellow?" Carroll asked.

"Ah," said Captain Ross. "These two appeared rather mysteriously on our ship."

"I'm Hopper." He held out a hand. They shook.

"And I'm Kaylie." She shook hands with Carroll, as well.

"So do you know where the island is?" Hopper asked.

Carroll laughed. "Yes, I know," he said. "Chief Timosofertu showed me, out of gratitude for me sharing Jesus with his people."

"Yes, it's a curious thing," Captain Ross said, glancing at Stede. "Hopper is an old friend of ours, and he has kind of an open invitation to stowaway aboard *The Robert Bruce*, but Kaylie here is a bit different. I don't know how she got aboard. Hopper doesn't know how she got aboard. And Kaylie herself claims not to know how she got aboard. Worse still, she had this scrap of parchment." He handed it to Carroll.

Carroll's eyes went wide when he read. "The spyglass!" he shouted. "How on earth do you know about the spyglass?"

Captain Ross's eyes narrowed. "We were hoping you might tell us."

"Me?" Carroll blanched. "I've never seen her before. And only the Brethren know of the spyglass. This very rhyme is one of a very few bits of lore that reveal its value." Father Carroll knelt to look Kaylie in the eye. "Please, child, tell us, how came you by this parchment?"

Kaylie sighed. She'd never felt so helpless. There was no way to explain what she was or how she'd ended up aboard the ship. There was no way to explain…anything. "I don't know," she said quietly. "I would tell you if I knew, but I don't."

Carroll stood. "There is more behind her words," he said. "But I think still she means well. There is no guile in her, nothing malicious at all."

"I feel the same," Ross said. "Now, then, Father Carroll, for the sake of your health and the people of Lakeba, I suggest we get you off the island."

"But...where will we go?"

"The Isle of Stars, of course," he said.

Carroll's posture tightened. "To the island...why?"

Ross crossed his arms. "I have a plan," he said. "There is no safe place to hide you from Dredd. He is determined, and well-financed. He won't stop looking for you, and I fear a fair number of your friends will suffer for it."

"Then what do you propose?"

"Dredd must be stopped. We must use his obsession against him, lure him to the island, where we'll be waiting."

"Use the treasure of the Isle of Stars...for bait?" Carroll looked sideways to Chief Timosofertu. "I cannot allow it. That island is a sacred place. We cannot risk its discovery to so foul a man as Tobias Dredd."

"He's already been there once," Ross said.

"Dredd? To the Isle of Stars? That cannot be so."

"It is," Ross explained. "But Dredd wasn't able to chart a course of any kind. It is a strange tale that I will relate to you once we're aboard *The Bruce*."

"Lead Tobias Dredd to the Isle of Stars?" Carroll echoed. "If we do so, and you cannot defeat him, he will rob the world of one of God's greatest creations."

"We will not let this happen," Ross replied.

"How can you be so sure?"

Ross glanced again at Stede. He laughed and said, "My confidence is not hubris. You must understand that I have some experience in matters such as these."

CHAPTER NINE

THE BROKEN SPYGLASS

Like the glowering bruise-colored mantle of a thundercloud hovering closer and closer but yet to release its first bolt of lightning, the atmosphere in the Lakeba village school hut became charged.

Kaylie tried to calm her nerves by drawing imaginary lines between the eyes of Father Carroll and Chief Timosofertu, Captain Ross and Stede as they exchanged glances. She saw red between Ross and Stede; blue between Carroll and the Chief. But, after many silent moments, the crisscrossing red and blue lines became a seriously tangled mess.

"Tell me, Captain Ross," Father Carroll said, breaking the stalemate. "Your interest in the Isle of Stars, is it purely an attempt to lure our enemy...or are there other reasons?"

"There are many reasons, Father," Ross explained. "I'll not deny them. Having seen the Isle of Swords, having held in my own hands the nails that crucified our Lord, I would see this Isle of Stars also. If it grants us even the smallest glimpse of heaven, then, I must see it for myself."

Carroll shifted his posture, looking more at ease but still determined. "And?"

"Rest easy, Carroll," Ross said. "We do not seek to plunder. While King George pays his Royal Navy precious little, the silver pinching brat, the crew of *The Robert Bruce* is still quite solvent. We've…uh, accrued quite a bit of wealth in our most recent adventures. The jewels upon the Isle of Stars are safe from our hands."

"That eases my heart," Father Carroll replied. "Lusts of the heart have been the ruin of many. There is wisdom in your plan, Captain Ross, and yet, I fear to risk the creation of Almighty God."

"If the island is not to be the bait, then you will be," Ross explained, his voice hardening. "And wherever you are, no one near you will be safe. Chief Timosofertu and his people are in terrible danger while you are here. If Dredd should—"

"We will fight dem!" Chief Timosofertu thundered. "We have turned our hearts to d'Christ, but we will defend our people, defend island. We fear not of Dredd."

"Chief Timosofertu, I offer you the highest respect for your stand," Ross said. "But that is precisely my point. The Lakebans will fight Dredd, and my crew would fight with them. We would defeat Dredd utterly; of this, I have no doubt, but at what cost? This village…this beautiful people, how many would perish in the effort? And for what? Jewels? Did not our Lord show us that people, all people, are worth so much more than things, even precious things? Are we to be like Judas objecting to the waste of priceless perfume on the feet of Christ?"

With a long, shuddering sigh, Father Carroll relented. "You remind me of the Apostle Paul, you know that?" he said with a sad laugh. "You are a former pirate, are you not? And yet, you lecture me from the Holy Scriptures. And there is great wisdom in your words. It seems to me that God is behind your visit."

"You think so?" Kaylie asked.

"Yes," Carroll replied. "For what purpose, I do not know. A trial…that much is clear." Carroll went to a desk in the back of the hut.

The desk was so beat up and warped Kaylie was surprised the drawers opened.

Carroll returned with a small telescope in his hand. "Behold," he said, "the broken spyglass." He handed it to Kaylie.

She looked through it at the inside of the hut. All she could see were odd shades of light and dark. "It's not working," she said, handing it to Hopper.

"That is why it is called the 'broken' spyglass," Carroll said.

Hopper tried to look through it. "Ah, it really doesn't work right," Hopper said. "What good is it if it's broken?"

Carroll took the telescope back. "Where is your faith, young Hopper?" he asked. He turned to Captain Ross and said, "As you know, The Isle of Stars is nearly impossible to find. But this spyglass makes it possible. Through its 'broken' lens, the island's jewels shine out with an odd blue light. By day, the spyglass filters the mist such that the landmass of the island itself can be seen. So you see, by day or night, this *broken* spyglass enables the island to be found."

"Amazing," whispered Captain Ross.

"Yes, indeed," Carroll said. He paused thoughtfully for a moment. "And now, about our departure?"

But no one answered. Explosions rocked the jungle. Villagers began shouting. Kaylie ducked. Hopper stared. The door to the hut opened and closed. Chief Timosofertu had vanished, but the lookout named Nock burst into the hut, followed by the other crewmen who'd come ashore.

"Captain Ross, thank the Almighty I've found you!" Nock yelled. "I knew the general direction you'd taken, but had to scour the jungle for your trail."

"What is it, Nock?" Ross asked. "Speak!"

"It's Old Toby, sir!" Nock said, his eyes bouncing from face to face. "His ship, *The Red Corsair*, has arrived at Lakeba, moored in a northern cove. But it's no mistake, Captain Dredd is here!"

Kaylie had never heard such noise in all her life. Even from inside the village hut, the sounds of men yelling, swords crashing together, and thundering explosions made Kaylie crouch down and cover her ears with her hands.

"Cat, Anne, protect the children!" Captain Ross shouted. "Get them back to the ship."

"Aye, Sir," Cat replied, drawing his sword.

"We'll keep them safe," Anne said, her sword already in hand.

"Carroll, gather your things quickly!" Captain Ross commanded. "You're coming with me."

"But the village," Carroll replied as he ran to the desk. "I won't just leave them. Dredd will kill them. I won't let that happen again." Carroll held up his multi-chambered flintlock pistol.

Captain Ross nodded. "I understand," he said. "These people are your family now. We will defend them, but stay close! We go on the count of three. One...two...THREE!"

Kaylie held Hopper's hand and watched Captain Ross, Father Carroll, and the others rush out from the hut.

Cat and Anne waited a few seconds. They turned to Kaylie and Hopper and yelled, "Now for it! Stay behind us!"

They charged out of the hut and, for Kaylie, it felt like everything slowed down. The clearing was full of fighting men. Pirates wearing red bandanas swarmed out of the forest like hornets.

They fired pistols at the villagers and attacked with swords. But the villagers stood their ground. They threw their spears, lifted their stone hatchets high, and ran right at the pirates. Others villagers burst from the foliage right behind the invaders, impaling them and dragging them with those polished hook weapons, dragging them back into the jungle.

Kaylie watched as Captain Ross, Father Carroll, and the man called Nock turned to the right when they left the hut. They met a group of pirates there.

Captain Ross and Nock swung their swords so fast that Kaylie could hardly follow the movement. Three pirates fell to the ground, but there were many more.

One pirate lifted his flintlock pistol and aimed at Captain Ross. Kaylie cried out.

There was a stunning white blur, a deafening explosion, and suddenly, the pirate and his pistol were simply gone. All that was left behind was a smoking ten-foot wide spread of blackened foliage.

"Ho, ho!" Jacques St. Pierre cried as he leaped over the smoldering mess. He patted his two remaining barrels of black powder. "Problem solved! Bon débarras!"

"That was close!" Cat shouted.

"Da, watch your flank!" Anne yelled.

"I'll be watchin' his flank!" Stede thundered. "St. Pierre just beat me to him, mon, dat's all."

"This way!" Cat cried, yanking Hopper. Anne took Kaylie's hand, and everything sped back up. Kaylie turned and ran, struggling to catch up. They raced behind the back of a hut.

"Wait," Cat urged. "I hear—"

Two pirates burst through the trees and attacked. Kaylie and Hopper ducked back behind Cat and Anne and huddled close to the rear of the hut.

Cat ducked one pirate's sword. Anne slashed that man's shoulder while Cat blocked the second pirate's cutlass with a swift parry of his own. Cat gave a quick twist and then lunged, flinging the pirate's sword from his hand. Cat punched the disarmed pirate so hard in the jaw that the man toppled into the foliage like a felled tree. Anne's opponent could barely lift his sword arm but, with his remaining hand, went for a pistol at his side. Anne's blinding slash removed that threat, and the man's arm at the elbow. She finished him with a savage kick to his throat.

Her ears still ringing from the explosion, Kaylie struggled with her own helplessness. As a Dreamtreader, she could have used her will to fight back. She could have saved the day. Now, she was nothing more than baggage.

Cat turned. "This way's no good!"

"We'll skirt the east side!" Anne cried out. "We'll come back to the ship from the hills."

Cat reached back for Hopper's hand, but in that moment, more enemy pirates crashed into the clearing.

"Look out!" Kaylie cried.

Cat spun but too late.

When Anne turned, her elbow hit Kaylie hard in side of her head. She fell to the ground, the ringing louder now, and gray clouds swirling in, closing her field of vision.

Kaylie saw two horrifying images before everything went black: One of the pirates lunged, catching Cat off guard and stabbing him. Another enemy grabbed Hopper and carried him off, kicking and screaming, into the Lakeban forest.

CHAPTER TEN

ABOARD THE RED CORSAIR

When Hopper woke up, he was laying down, in the dark. The last thing he remembered was being grabbed and dragged through the jungle by a pirate who smelled like a combination of bad fish and sewer gas.

But where am I now? he wondered. It smelled better at least. Some kind of raw wood, pine maybe.

For a moment, he thought maybe he was back aboard *The Robert Bruce*. It wouldn't be the first time he'd fallen asleep in a ship's hold and had extraordinarily realistic dreams. "Kaylie," he whispered. "Kaylie?"

There was no answer. Hopper felt around and got a splinter for his trouble. There was wood close around him on all sides. He wriggled his shoulders. Very close. He tried to sit up and bonked his head. Too close.

"Hey!" he cried out. "Who put me in a box?" He kicked out, and something moved. He kicked harder and harder until finally, a long top popped off and slid to the side. Hopper sat up and saw the true nature of the box that had imprisoned him. A coffin. He'd been left in a wooden coffin and, as he gazed around, he found his coffin was one among many.

"Eww!" Hopper shouted. "Who put me in a coffin? I'm not dead!"

"Cavendish!" someone shouted. "That lad's not dead after all!"

"I just said that!" Hopper grumbled as he leaped out the coffin.

A pirate with three gold rings in his nose grabbed Hopper's arm. "Here now," said the pirate. "Calm down, calm down. It's just me, old Cavendish. You're out."

Hopper looked around. He found himself in a lantern-lit room, deep in the bowels of a ship. Three other pirates stood around, faces twisted in variations of surprise. Cavendish still held his arm. And that's when the smell hit Hopper. It was something like an old compost pile mixed with a sopping wet dog.

Hopper gagged and shook himself free. "Why did you put me in...in there?" Hopper asked.

"Oh, sorry lad," said Cavendish. "But ye conked out on me as we run in from the island. Ye didn't move. I figured ye for dead."

"Where's my friend, Kaylie?" Hopper asked. "You didn't put her in a coffin too, did you?"

"Girl?" Cavendish asked. "I didn't see no girl."

"She was right next to me," Hopper said. "How'd you miss her?"

"I dunno, lad," Cavendish replied. "Easy to miss things when ye be fightin' fer yer life. Girl's still on Lakeba then, I guess."

One of the other pirates, a bent man with black slanted eyebrows and pointy ears, said, "We best be takin' the lad to see the captain, then."

"Right away, Mister Kilgore," Cavendish said. "Right away. But it's yer turn to disturb the captain."

"Bloody ain't!" Kilgore snapped.

"Who told'im 'bout *The Robert Bruce* bein' in port?"

"Ah, rat scat," Kilgore muttered. "Right ye are, my turn is up an' more's the misery." He grabbed Hopper's shoulder and shoved him past the coffins to a little aisle that ran between a few dozen open barrels. Hopper stumbled into the pathway and saw something very strange. Some of the open barrels were full of hundreds of dark red flowering plants.

"Are…are those roses?" Hopper asked.

"Yeah," said Kilgore, continuing to steer Hopper through the barrels. A ladder jutted down from a darkened hatch in the bulkhead. "Roses are the captain's favorite."

Cavendish laughed and said, "Just pray that Captain Dredd don't give ye one."

Hopper swallowed and climbed the ladder. Kilgore called down, "You louts be sure to give'm water at second bell."

"Yeah, yeah," Cavendish groused back. "I'd sooner be pickled and fed to sharks than shirk the captain's bloody flowers."

Hopper swallowed again, poking his eyes up above the hatch. Up on deck, oil lanterns hung from every mast and kept away the night. A snapping sound drew Hopper's eyes. He saw a huge black flag whipped by the wind this side of the mainsail. Emblazoned with a grinning pale skull upon crisscrossed long stem red roses, the flag was an ominous puzzle. For whatever the symbols meant, Hopper thought, it couldn't be anything but sinister. Hulking iron cannons waited dangerously in long rows by each side rail, and rigging lines hung down from spars like so many hangman's nooses.

Kilgore pushed Hopper up out of the hatch and along the deck. They stopped abruptly behind a very large man who wore a black coat that hung all the way down to his boots.

"A little surprise for ye, Captain," Kilgore said.

"Can't you see I am busy here?" the captain roared. Then, he turned around.

Hopper took a step backward and bumped into Kilgore.

Captain Tobias Dredd was dressed all in black, from his hat, vest, bandolier, shirt, trousers, gloves, and boots—all as black as squid ink. But he had a single red rose pinned to the lapel of his coat. He also wore a long, curved sword. Hopper had seen many swords, both military and pirate, but this one looked unique. Its blade was thinner than those of most cutlass swords, and it had two grooves running its length, not one. And its hilt seemed to be some sort of bluish black, wrought iron basket.

Frightening as the sword was, it was the man's face that set Hopper to trembling. Captain Dredd had large, bloodshot eyes. His tiny sneering mouth was surrounded by a thin mustache and greasy little patch of a beard. Those rage-filled eyes and that ruthless sneer—before them, Hopper felt worthless, like some insect to be squashed and swept away.

"Who is this…child?" Dredd asked.

"Cavendish brought him aboard," Kilgore said.

"Why?" asked Captain Dredd.

Kilgore pulled nervously at one of his pointed ears. "I dunno, Captain," he said. "I guess he didn't want to leave 'im with those savages. 'Fraid they might eat him."

"He is your problem," Captain Dredd said. "Not mine. Now, I have work to do."

As Captain Dredd turned away, Hopper saw the missionary Father Carroll. And he was tied to one of the ship's masts.

"Father Carroll!" Hopper yelled. "Are you alright?"

Father Carroll blinked. He leaned his head a bit and said, "Don't worry about me, Hopper. I'm sorry you got mixed up in this."

"The missionary would be just fine," said Captain Dredd, "if he would just tell me how to get to the Starlight Isle."

"I can't!" Carroll said. "I told you. I left the broken spyglass on Lakeba."

Captain Dredd shook his head. "I know you better than that," he said. "You are a sailor. You can find the island by the stars, can't you?"

Father Carroll did not answer.

"I thought so," Captain Dredd said. He drew his sword. "Now, plot me a course to the island!"

"Never," Carroll said. "Starlight Isle is a wonder of God's creation. I won't have you destroying it!"

Captain Dredd held the point of his sword to the missionary's chin. "In a few moments," Captain Dredd said, "you will do whatever I ask."

"Just tell him!" Hopper shouted. "I don't want you to get hurt!"

"Listen to the child," Captain Dredd said. "He is wise. What riches are worth your blood?"

"My blood is worth nothing compared to God's creation," Carroll said. "Just kill me. Get it over with."

Captain Dredd laughed. "No," he said. "I won't kill you. It's bad luck to kill a holy man. But that doesn't mean I can't torture you a bit. Kilgore, take the child below. Tell Cavendish to fetch my whip."

CHAPTER ELEVEN

THE ISLE OF STARS

The next morning, Hopper woke up in a cold, barred cell below decks on Captain Dredd's ship, *The Red Corsair*. He was glad to be alive but, just as soon as he opened his eyes, echoes of whip cracks and screams bombarded him like cannon fire. Hopper hunched over, held his head in his hands, and wept.

"Ah, now don't ye worry, lad," Cavendish said, appearing at the cell door and carrying a small tray of bread, cheese, and salted meat. "That old priest, well, I suppose he's had better days. But he seems made of stronger stuff than first meets the eye."

"Captain Dredd won't kill him, will he?" Hopper asked.

Cavendish picked thoughtfully at something stuck between his brownish teeth. "No, not a'purpose," Cavendish said, sliding the tray of food under Hopper's cell door. "I think Cap'n Dredd respects Carroll, I do. Strength, wisdom, and a bit a' gall—that priest's got all a' that. Naw, Dredd won't be droppin' a rose on Carroll."

Drop a rose? Hopper wondered. "What do you mean?"

"See that's Captain Dredd's thing," Cavendish said. "We attack other ships, ye see, and takes what they got. Sometimes, it goes smooth like. Other's not so much, and we need to do a fair amount a' killin'. Whenever Dredd kills the other ship's captain, he leaves a rose on deck. It's like a signature…and a warning."

Cavendish gave a kind of cringing shrug, a weak, sideways smile, and then left Hopper alone in his cell. Hopper thought about the poor missionary. He thought about Kaylie back on Lakeba Island. Then he prayed for them all.

Some time later, Hopper woke up again, but this time, in the dark. He heard something. There was someone else in the cell.

"I have failed," Father Carroll groaned.

Hopper found the missionary lying on his stomach across a long bench. "Father Carroll?" Hopper whispered. "Father Carroll, are you...are you hurt?" Soon as he'd said it, Hopper knew it was a foolish question. Even in the dark, Hopper could see the dark stain on the back of Carroll's shirt.

"I will live," Carroll said, rolling slightly. He grunted and rose up onto his elbow and side. "And that is more than I deserve for such a collapse."

Hopper dipped a cloth into a bucket of water and held it to the man's forehead. "I don't think you failed," Hopper said.

"But I told him," Carroll said. "I plotted his course to the Isle of Stars. Now Dredd and his greedy crew will ruin it. They will destroy the beauty God created."

"They can't destroy an island, can they?" Hopper asked.

"You...you haven't seen the island, Hopper," Carroll said. "The jewels so bright...so many colors. And from the mountain, the view...it is breathtaking."

"Maybe he won't take all the jewels," Hopper said.

"Ah, Hopper, you have a good heart," Carroll said. "But you do not know Captain Tobias Dredd. Wherever he goes, blood, fire, and destruction are sure to follow."

"But even bad men can change," Hopper said. "The Apostle Paul did."

Carroll laughed, then groaned in pain. "Ah, to think I am the minister," Carroll said. "And yet, you give me lessons in faith. It seems everyone is teaching me these days. Still, I'm afraid it would take a mighty blow to crack Dredd's hard heart."

"I dunno, Guv'nor," Hopper said, "but aren't you forgettin' Declan Ross and the crew of *The Robert Bruce*?"

"What do you mean?"

"He had a plan, right? To bait Captain Dredd and then catch him at the Isle of Stars?"

With another groan, Father Carroll sat up on the bench. "Oh, lad, I'm not altogether certain that Ross is still alive. Dredd's attack on Lakeba was so sudden and swift. I know we were not pursued as *The Red Corsair* departed the island. And now, even if Ross and his crew were at full strength, they'd never find the Isle of Stars. I'm afraid—"

Just then, the whole ship shook. Several loud voices cried out way up on deck.

"C'mon, you louts!" Kilgore shouted. He came down the ladder with a blazing torch in his hand and ten other pirates following. With the blazing torch and his pointed ears, Kilgore looked like a devil. "We've come at last to the Starlight Isle, and Captain Dredd be wantin' ye topside."

Kilgore opened the cell. Surrounded by the pirates, Carroll and Hopper made their way up on deck. It was still very much night outside, but which night? Hopper couldn't tell. *How long has it been since Lakeba?* he wondered.

Kilgore and the other men pushed Hopper and Father Carroll to the port rail, joining many others in staring across the dark sea. *There must be some mistake,* Hopper thought. He leaned on the rail and stared. Millions of startlingly bright stars dotted the eggplant blue sky. Silver ripples danced upon the undulating black waters. But no land.

Hopper squinted and caught his tongue between his lips, trying to think the mystery through. "Father Carroll," Hopper muttered. "All I see before me are stars and sea. Are you certain there's an island there?"

"Yes!" someone answered, but it wasn't Father Carroll. Tobias Dredd came forward. His bloodshot eyes glinted in the torchlight. And a cruel smile curled on his lips. "At last, I return to the Starlight Island!"

"Return?" Father Carroll blurted out. "Declan Ross said as much, but I don't believe God would permit such as you to see His wonder."

"Bite your tongue, holy man," Dredd growled. "You speak in ignorance."

Hopper said, "I still don't see anything out there."

"Nor would you," Captain Dredd explained. "It is impossible to see at night until you are right on top of it. And then, it is too late. You will crash into sharp reefs beneath the water."

Father Carroll gasped and said, "You know...about the reefs?"

Captain Dredd laughed but did not answer. "Drop the cutters!" Dredd shouted.

The pirates went to work. They lowered several six-man boats into the water and began to board them. Carroll and Hopper rode with Captain Dredd. Three other pirates did the rowing.

Hopper looked over the side and saw pale shapes just a few feet under the surface. "What are those?" Hopper asked.

"Fins of coral," Father Carroll said. "Very sharp. They will break a tall ship to bits."

"I can attest to that," Captain Dredd said. "The year was 1808, and I was about as old as this urchin here." He pointed to Hopper. "My mother often took me on sailing trips upon these waters in her ship, a square-rigged brig called *The Spanish Rose*. Heh, heh, she was quite the pirate herself."

His mum was a pirate? Hopper thought. That drew his mind back to his adoptive parents, Brandon and Dolphin Blake, and the reality of his situation fell like a heavy weight upon his shoulders. *I may never see them again,* he thought.

"We got off course in a storm," Captain Dredd continued. "When the sky cleared, my mother couldn't read the charts correctly. The stars on the horizon were strange. The ship's quartermaster, a heartless rogue named Morlan, led a mutiny against my mother. Before the bloody fight was settled, we ran aground, impaling ourselves upon the reef."

Father Carroll looked up suddenly. "I...I never knew."

Captain Dredd opened his coat and took out a beautiful red rose.

Oh, no! Hopper thought. *He's going to kill us.*

But Captain Dredd made no move for his sword. He just held the rose and kept talking. "My mother did not survive the crash, and I barely did," he said. "We floated on two different pieces of wreckage. The last thing I remember is watching my mother float away...that, and an island made of stars."

"That's terrible," Hopper said.

Captain Dredd nodded. "The rose was always her favorite flower," he said, staring across the dark water. "It was more than the rich, crimson beauty, though. She said roses reminded her of better times."

"Roses," Father Carroll whispered.

"Yes," Dredd hissed. "Blood. Red. Roses. Like this one, like the ones crossed on my black flag, and like those I leave behind—all for her."

"And so," Father Carroll said, "you've chosen to honor her memory by stealing and murdering...and leaving roses behind?"

He snorted with anger. "What do you know, priest? Ah, but no matter! At least now I return to the island to take its riches, to claim what this wicked world owes me...at last!"

He is going to steal the jewels, Hopper thought. Carroll was right. But then Hopper looked up, and suddenly, there it was. An island made of stars.

He could just barely see the outline of the dark gray sandy shore. Nearly black mountain ridges rose up all around it. But as their cutter boat slid up onto the sand, all Hopper could do was stare. It was as if stars had come to rest on the island. In the sand, in the stone, everywhere: huge gems of electric blue or white.

Hopper watched Captain Dredd go ashore. The pirate captain leaned over, dug in the sand, and picked up a bright gem the size of an apple.

It glowed with white light and showered Captain Dredd's tired face with many sparkles. He wandered around the sand. The rose dangled in his other hand.

More pirate groups began to arrive on the shore. And no sooner did they drag their cutters onto the sand than they began gathering up the shining jewels. Kilgore leaped around like a crazy man, stuffing his sack with every gem he could find.

"Stop!" Father Carroll cried. "There are no other islands like this one in all the world! This is God's creation, the last remnant of Eden!"

"Silent, holy man!" Captain Dredd yelled. "If this island is what's left of perfection, then it is just that I ruin it. We will take from God precisely what he took from me!"

"God did not cause that wreck," Father Carroll said.

Dredd muttered, "Tell that to my dead mother."

Carroll was still a moment. Then, he looked up suddenly. "Wait, Dredd!" he shouted. He ran up to the captain.

Dredd drew his curved sword and placed the tip against Carroll's chest. Hopper gasped.

"You will not hinder me," Captain Dredd snarled.

"I doubt there's anything I can do to hinder you," Carroll said. "But remember, I've been to this island many, many times. I know its terrain. I know its secrets. And I think there's something else here. Something that you should see."

CHAPTER TWELVE

THE CHASE

When Kaylie awoke, she was lying on a cot inside a ship, in a long, narrow cabin where other bunks as thin as hers jutted out from the walls on both sides. A dumpy-looking man dressed all in white waddled around the room, his walrus-tusk mustache whipping back behind his jaw as he darted quickly from bed to bed. And Kaylie noted grimly that the other beds were not empty. They were wounded, men from *The Robert Bruce*, as well as natives from Lakeba, most of them wrapped in bloody bandages. Some were deathly still, while others writhed, groaning or muttering.

The dumpy man seemed to be some sort of doctor, for he carried a black leather satchel in one hand. Kaylie sat up sharply. This man had only one hand. His other arm ended at the elbow with a knobby stump.

"Oh, sir!" Kaylie called out. "You lost your arm on the island, in the battle? I'm so sorry."

"What?" the man balked, spinning on his heel. "Oh, there now, lass, yer awake at last. Took a nasty knock on the noggin, ye did."

"But, but your arm?"

"What? Oh, this?" He waved his short arm around and laughed. "Nah, miss, I lost this a ways back. Wasn't even on the island to fight. Good thing, too, or else, who'd a' looked after all you folk?" He laughed again, but it was a polite thing, drained of any real mirth. "I'm Nubby, the ship's doctor, uh…and cook."

Kaylie blinked a few times. The rest of the memories came flooding back in: the pirate's lunge, Cat going down to one knee, and the other man snatching up Hopper and racing off with him as if he were a sack of grain. "Oh, no," she said sadly. "It's not supposed to be like this. His books always have happy endings. It's all gone wrong."

Nubby eyed her with concern written across his brow. "Perhaps, ye ought to lay down again for a bit," he suggested gently. "Yer not making a bit of sense."

Kaylie shook her head. "But it has all gone wrong," she said, swiping at the hot tears trickling on either side of her nose. "Hasn't it? Dredd's men, they've taken Hopper, haven't they? And poor Cat. They've killed him."

Nubby sidled up to her bedside. "No, lass, no," he said. "Cat's took a blade to the shoulder, but he'll be fine. From what I hear, the pirate he was fighting didn't do quite so well. Nah, Cat wouldn't be had so easy, miss. He's fiercer than his namesake, that one. No cat 'o nine tails ever fought so nimbly."

Kaylie blinked back more tears. "He's okay?"

Nubby nodded. "Up on deck with Anne and Captain Ross, I'll wager."

"And Hopper? Did he, well, did anyone rescue him?"

"He wasn't among the wounded," Nubby replied. "That's my charge, miss, so I'm afraid I don't know what became of Hopper."

Kaylie swallowed and looked down at herself. "I don't see any blood on me," she mumbled. "Am I…am I okay?"

Nubby tugged on one side of his long mustache and said, "Like I said, ya took a wicked whack to the head. How do ye feel?"

"A little hungry," she replied. "And sad."

"Hunger I can help with," Nubby said. "See that ladder there? It'll take ya one deck up. Hop off there, head port side. You'll find the galley. Help yourself to the vittles."

Kaylie shoved herself off the cot, tested her balance, found it good enough, and took the ladder up. She found a tin full of hard biscuits and a jar of honey. She took a biscuit, slathered it until it glistened in the torchlight, and then munched it all the way to the main deck.

She found that it was night. Scores of Captain Ross's sailors raced to and fro, all over the deck, like ants from an anthill that had just been kicked over. Some sailors attended to heavy cannons, pushing them into place near the ship's side rails. Others carried huge rolled-up pieces of cloth. *Sails,* Kaylie thought, but they were all torn up.

Kaylie felt a hand on her shoulder and turned. It was Captain Ross. His hazel eyes twinkled with kindness. "Good to see you up and about," he said. "Are you well?"

Kaylie swallowed the last bit of honeyed biscuit. "I guess so," she said. "What's going on?"

"Captain Dredd put men on our ship and tore up our sails," Captain Ross said. "Good thing for us, I had spare sails below."

"Captain, what happened?" Kaylie asked. "Where's Hopper? Where's Father Carroll?"

"Both still alive as far as I know," Captain Ross said. "But Dredd took them."

"Oh, no," Kaylie said. "Does that mean—"

"Don't you worry, lass," Captain Ross said. "We'll get them back."

"But how?" Kaylie cried. "Captain Dredd's going to the Isle of Stars. And we'll never find it."

"Oh, we might," Captain Ross said. He pulled something out of his jacket.

"The broken telescope!" Kaylie shouted. "I can't believe it."

"Yes," the captain said. "And more than that. We have Chief Timo!" He pointed to the poop deck, and there was the chief of the Lakeba natives. His wild hair blew every which way in the sea winds. "With the spyglass and Timo's help, we are gaining even now on the *Red Corsair.*"

Hours passed. Chief Timosofertu, Captain Ross, Cat, Anne, and Stede huddled together over maps and star charts. From time to time, Kaylie saw the captain look through the broken spyglass.

A moment later, Cat and Anne wandered to Kaylie's side. Cat's left arm was wrapped in a sling. "Glad to see you," Cat said to Kaylie. "Seems as though I'd better be a good husband. I wouldn't want to get a hard elbow from Anne like she gave you."

"Hey!" Anne feigned indignation, giving him a light slap on the shoulder.

"Not that shoulder, please," Cat groaned.

"Oh, sorry," Anne replied with a grimace.

Kaylie smiled weakly. "Anne didn't hit me so hard," she said. "I'm just worried about Hopper and Father Carroll."

"I understand," Cat said. "I'm worried also. But, from what I've learned about Captain Tobias Dredd, he's not a reckless killer. Not like my f—well, not like some other pirates. Dredd kills when others hinder him or get in his way. I can't imagine Hopper being much of a threat to him."

"But what about Father Carroll?"

Cat didn't answer. Anne did. "Let us hope and pray for the best, Kaylie. My father and this crew will do everything we can to get our people back safely. And we will see to it that—"

"I SEE IT!!" Captain Ross yelled from the wheel.

Kaylie, Cat, and Anne climbed the stairs to the quarterdeck where the captain steered the ship.

"The island?" Kaylie asked. "Isle of Stars?" She looked out to sea but saw nothing but stars.

Captain Ross handed her the spyglass. She put it to her eyes. Right away the stars and sea looked very different.

The sky was a deep purple with golden stars. The sea was very dark blue. And between the two, a black island full of white sparkles appeared.

"I see it!" Kaylie shouted. "This is amazing."

Captain Ross gently took the telescope from Kaylie. "Sorry, lass," he said. "But I need this now. Chief Timo tells me that we can't get too close. Reefs there will wreck us."

Kaylie wondered if Captain Dredd had already come to the island. She hoped that he hadn't struck the reef...for Hopper's sake anyway. She didn't wonder for long.

"Looks like Old Toby's already here," Captain Ross said. He handed the spyglass to Chief Timo.

Chief Timo said, "Sail ship to west side of island. We come in. Dredd no see us."

Captain Ross guided the ship in a wide half-circle and, once they were positioned adjacent to the island's western shore, he dropped anchor. "Launch the cutters!" Captain Ross shouted.

Kaylie saw Red Eye leap over a rail and begin to clamber down a rope ladder. She went to follow. But Captain Ross held up a hand. "Hold, where do you think you're going?"

"Well, to the isle, of course," Red Eye said.

"Not you, ye lout," Ross said. "You, Miss Kaylie?"

"I'm going too," she replied quietly.

"That, Miss Kaylie, would be a remarkably bad idea," said the captain. "I've put you in danger enough, and while it was nothing grave, you've been injured. You stay on the ship."

"Captain Ross, I can't stay here," Kaylie said. "Hopper's out there somewhere. I need to help if I can."

"Forgive my saying," said the captain, "but you're just a girl. And there's right nasty pirates out there."

"I've heard that speech many times," Anne said, appearing at her father's side. Cat was right behind her. "Too many times."

Declan Ross huffed. "You're one to speak, daughter," he said. "When I let Kaylie and Hopper ashore at Lakeba, you'll recall I tasked you and Cat to keep them safe. And what happened?"

Anne looked away.

"That's not quite fair, Captain," Cat replied. "We were taken by surprise."

"Exactly my point," Ross replied. "If there's anything that can be expected on the Isle of Stars, it's the unexpected. I won't risk Kaylie's well-being again. It's not about her being a girl. She's a child. And it's not about your skill to protect her, nor Anne's. No one can protect her from every possible danger."

"God can," Kaylie said. "Please, Captain Ross, let me go. I don't know how I ended up on your ship. I don't know where the parchment about the spyglass came from. I don't understand any of this, but I feel that I belong here now. God meant me to be here, and I feel that I need to see it through to whatever end."

"To whatever end, eh?" Ross replied, thoughtfully scratching at his chin.

"Besides, I've been in some pretty tough places before," Kaylie said. "Places you wouldn't believe."

Captain Ross eyed her for some time. "Who am I to stand in the way of the Almighty's plans," he said at last. "But I don't like this. I don't like this one bit. You'll go to the island if you must, but stay away from the fighting. Cat and Anne, you'll keep her safe, better than last time, hear?"

"Yes, Da," Anne said.

"Yes, Captain," Cat replied.

"Anythin' else fer me, Cap'n?" Red Eye growled from the rail.

"Nothing more," Captain Ross said. "But, Red Eye, you remember our agreement. You'll follow it to the letter."

Red Eye gave the slightest of nods and then raced down the rope ladder to a cutter.

"Right then," Ross said. "Cat, Anne, and Kaylie, I want you in a different cutter and, once on shore, I'll want you as far away from Red Eye as possible."

"Understood," Cat replied.

Kaylie was amazed at how quickly Captain Ross's men rowed the long boats. They came to shore in no time.

And what a shore it was.

For several minutes, Captain Ross, Cat, Anne, Stede, Red Eye, and the others stood like statues. Then, they wandered from one bright, sparkling gem to another.

Captain Ross said, "I never imagined in my wildest dreams there could be so many. I never thought it would be so beautiful."

Kaylie reached down and plucked an orange-sized jewel from the sand easily. It was so gloriously bright that she could barely look at it. She held it up with both hands for the others to see.

"It's…it's right wonderful, it is," Red Eye said.

"C'est magnifique!" shouted Jacques St. Pierre. "It is like zee beauty and fury of an explosion, but without zee BOOM!"

"Dat be d'mos stunnin' jewel, mon," Stede said.

"Even among the treasures in the vaults of the Isle of Swords," Ross said quietly, "I've not seen the like."

Chief Timo pointed. "Dredd there!" he shouted. They all looked up. Quite a distance away, torches snaked up the mountainside like a serpent of fire.

"Right, then!" Captain Ross called. "Much as I'd like to stay and stare, we have a job here. People to save, Dredd's pirates to defeat, and one of God's wonders to protect."

Once all of his men were on shore, Captain Declan Ross led the way. They marched across the long shore and then over black rock. And finally, they cut their way into patches of dark forest.

Kaylie kept up as best she could. She leaned out here and there and saw the torches were getting closer.

"It's time we stay back a bit," Cat said. "Duck down here with me."

Captain Ross drew his cutlass sword. "Come on men! Now to it!"

They charged out of the forest and up the slope. Captain Dredd's pirates dropped their crates full of glowing jewels. They drew swords, and some of them raised musket rifles.

Captain Ross drove his sword through one pirate. One of Dredd's men fired his rifle. But Captain Ross held the dead pirate up like a shield. More shots rang out. Steel met steel all over the black rocky slope.

"The sound is awful," Kaylie said. "Worse than Lakeba."

"I don't like it either, miss," Anne said. "We'll fight like lions, but Dredd's men...they have the advantage."

"What?" Kaylie asked. "Why?"

Anne put a hand on Kaylie's shoulder. "They have the higher ground."

CHAPTER THIRTEEN

THE CLIMB

"Where are you taking me, holy man?" Captain Dredd demanded. He thrust his blazing torch within a foot of the priest's face. "I don't care much for heights."

Father Carroll reeled back from the flame. "It's not much farther!" he yelped. *Lord, help me, that torch is an inferno!* he thought. "Now, please, move that raging brand. I'm rather fond of my eyebrows."

"You have pluck for a priest," Dredd replied, adjusting the angle of his torch so that Carroll could continue on the path.

Carroll muttered, "Just a few more minutes' climb."

"You mean a few more minutes of hacking and climbing," Dredd groused. He pointed his narrow, basket-hilted sword forward, gesturing just ahead to Kilgore.

The man was a machete-wielding storm in the shadows, mercilessly crashing into the dense foliage. "I would think," Kilgore grumbled, spitting and coughing, "you'd know an easier way if you'd been to this *secret* place before."

"I...I have," Carroll said, pausing to pick bits of leaf matter out of his own hair. "But, among all the wonders of this island, I visit this...place...least. I don't know why, but this destination has always felt to me that it should remain unspoiled."

"It's sure enough goin' t'be spoiled now, mahn," boomed the West Indian pirate who clambered behind the priest. He gave Father Carroll a shove forward with one massive hand. With the other, he dragged Hopper along behind him.

He sounds like Stede, Hopper thought. *Doesn't look much like him though.*

The huge, shirtless, dark-skinned man wore lizard skin breeches. At his waist, he had a blood red sash, partially hiding the thick black belt and huge golden buckle beneath. He wore a necklace of tarnished coins on his muscular neck. His head was clean-shaven, but a wicked scar scored an hourglass groove from his forehead, over his massive overhanging brow, and down beneath his glowering eyes. "I grow weary of dis climb," he growled. "Wid each step, we b'gettin' farther from d'treasure."

"Our ideas of treasure, big man," Carroll said, "are vastly different."

"I wouldn't upset old Bastian here," Dredd warned with a vicious laugh. "He may not look it but, when angered, he can get a bit mean spirited. He breaks things."

Hopper swallowed, imagining it well: *If the brute had a mind to, he could snap me like a pile of bone-dry sticks.*

The mood darkened from there. In spite of the incredible flickering canopy of stars overhead, there was no thought for beauty. The climb steepened. Kilgore's machete strokes slowed. He cursed and spat and cursed some more.

Carroll himself paused, seemingly uncertain about the path. "Wait," he said. "Bah, I did this once before. It fools you, this terrain. The foliage gets thinner, makes the way easier, but it is not the true way."

Kilgore slammed the machete into the trunk of a fat palm. "What, pray, is the true way?" he spat.

"We've got to go through there," Carroll explained, pointing into a seemingly impenetrable thicket. "On the other side, the path curls up and east, a precarious climb."

"What?" Kilgore objected. "Through that wall a' green?"

"You had better not be planning some fool stunt," Captain Dredd said. "You won't get close enough to me to push me off a cliff."

"I promise you, I have no such plans," Carroll said. "I want you to see this, a view like no other in the world. It is a gift from God to mankind."

"And a great many jewels, you said," Captain Dredd said. "I care nothing for views."

Hopper wasn't so sure about that. He'd seen the look on Captain Dredd's face when they first came to Starlight Isle.

"Thousands of jewels," Carroll said, "more than any other place on the island."

"Jewels is jewels," Kilgore muttered, pointing far below at the crescent shoreline. "Might as well have the easy ones down there. My machete's sharp, but there be no getting through this thick mess."

Hopper wondered what the missionary was up to. They were getting pretty high up on the mountain. *Wait!* Hopper thought. *He's stalling Captain Dredd, hoping that Captain Ross will come.* Hopper thought sure that was it.

"Stand aside!" Bastian growled, barreling past Carroll. He snatched up Kilgore's machete and charged at the wall of green. His left arm, so segmented with muscle that it looked like it belonged to some enormous crab, went up and crashed down like a felled tree.

The resultant splintering cracks startled Hopper. He ducked and covered his ears. Still, he couldn't help watching Bastian work.

The giant swept his right arm and took out the stalks and trunks he'd severed with the machete, thrusting them aside like a panel of bamboo. Bastian worked with a kind of sway. He reared back to the left. Down came the machete. Then he twisted his torso and swept the wreckage away. *Chop, crack, whoosh!*

In a few moments, Bastian had left a trail of destruction curving in his wake.

"Don't just stand there, gaping like baboons," Dredd commanded. "You louts, go help him."

Kilgore stumbled ahead. Then, Hopper smelled something foul. It was like a mixture of fresh manure and stagnant swamp water. The pirate called Cavendish hurried by him to catch up with Bastian.

"Come," Carroll said, taking Hopper's hand. "It's not far now."

Angry orange light flashed behind them both, and Dredd was there with his torch. "Go on," he hissed. "Keep in front...where I can see you."

They clambered through Bastian's destruction, climbed an upward spiral until their calves ached. And then, they nearly crashed into Cavendish, Kilgore, and Bastian, in that order.

"I almost ran you through!" Dredd spat. "Why have you stopped?"

Bastian's broad shoulders shuddered. "No place to go, mahn," he said, his voice low and flat.

"For your sake, Carroll," Dredd muttered, "he'd better be wrong. Speak plainly, Bastian."

"There's...there's...a cave," Kilgore said, his words coming in breathy gasps.

"You've never seen the like," Cavendish whispered.

"What's this nonsense?" Dredd growled. "We've explored the caves of a hundred islands. Bastian, you especially know this sort of terrain."

"Not like this, mahn," Bastian replied.

Dredd let out a guttural grunt and charged forward. "Stand aside, then!"

Kilgore and Cavendish slid to the left. Bastian slid right.

Dredd froze in his tracks.

CHAPTER FOURTEEN

THE CAVE

Near the top of the isle's elevation, a gaping black mouth opened in a face of scaly, striated gray limestone. All was not darkness within, but what light there was came from wisps of smoky luminescence, twisting along the cave floor, dancing upon the curving contours of the ceiling, or even writhing in the air at eye level.

"Dat be a jumbee cave," Bastian whispered. "And I'll not be goin' inside."

"Jumbee?" Hopper asked.

"Spirits," Bastian gravely explained, stepping another pace back from the cave's mouth. "And all o'dem d'mos evil sort. We mus' stay away, dat be true."

"You'll go if I command it," Dredd snarled through his teeth.

"Many years past, I be true to you, mahn," Bastian said. "I been d'mahn you can trust when all else fails, but 'dis...'dis you cannot make me do."

Hopper stared into cave's mouth. The tendrils of light swirled and then dissipated, only to reappear a moment later, some distance away. More than once, Hopper fancied that he'd seen a face in the pale smoke, a leering, undulating face. "Spirits," he whispered.

"They are no such thing," Father Carroll said firmly. "The misty lights are a mere trick of the rare geological make-up of The Isle of

Stars. There is something luminous in the minerals here, causing both the gems, and these strange vapors, to glow."

"I don't like this," Captain Dredd muttered. He stood by the opening of the cave. "You are up to something, aren't you, Christian?"

"Only a fool would try to mislead you," Carroll said. "I am not so much a fool as that but, lest you still doubt me, I give my solemn word that there is no danger within the cave. If I lie, I would betray my Lord as well. I could never do that."

"I don't know, sir," Kilgore said. "Something unnatural at work here."

Cavendish shrugged. "Maybe," he said. "Maybe not. Seems to me the priest steered us right so far."

Captain Dredd stepped backward suddenly and grabbed Hopper by the shoulder. "I trust the word of no man," Dredd fumed. "Especially not a priest. We'll let the boy go first into the cave. If you have something ill planned for me, Christian, if there is some hidden trap, the boy will suffer first."

"No, mahn," Bastian cried out, his voice thin with fear. "D'chile cannot enter. D'jumbees do outrageous horror to d'child. To mahn too, but especially to d'child."

"There are no jumbees," Father Carroll said, kneeling close to Hopper. "What you see inside the mouth of this cave is yet another example of God's glorious creation. Turn away thoughts of evil spirits or monsters. There is nothing impure upon this island, lest man bring it with him. Don't worry."

Don't worry? Easy for you to say, thought Hopper. He took a few steps toward the cave. Watching the glowing wisps dance and swirl was terrifying, mesmerizing, and…almost beautiful. The longer he looked, the more incredible the vision before him grew. The whirling vapors seemed to be just three luminous colors: purple, blue, and white. But within those three main hues, there were a vast variety of shades and degrees of brightness. They appeared and vanished with no distinguishable pattern like shooting stars, and Hopper found a smile forming upon his lips as he tried in vain to guess where one might appear next.

"You see?" Carroll asked. "There is nothing to fear. Go on, Hopper, show these fearsome pirates what real courage looks like."

"That your idea of Christian charity?" Dredd jeered. "I almost cannot believe it. You really are going to let the boy go first."

"There is nothing for any of us to fear in that cave," Carroll shot back. "Not unless you fear that which is good, as many men do. In any case, Hopper will be far safer inside than he would be within your reach, Dredd."

Hopper grinned at that. *Score one for Father Carroll,* he thought as he took a few more tentative steps toward the cave. The stone roof above his head seemed to eat up the sky. And the shadows within seemed to reach out to him, to embrace him, to gather him inside. Soon, the dancing vapors were all around him, startling him as they blinked into existence.

"Hey, Guv'nor!" he cried. "I can feel them. It's like breaths of air or the touch of feathers. Sort of tickles, like."

Father Carroll smiled.

Bastian rocked back and forth on his heels, staring goggle-eyed after Hopper as if he expected the lad to be grabbed up, torn to pieces, or burned alive.

Kilgore, Cavendish, and Captain Dredd watched closely too, silent until Hopper disappeared from sight.

"What happened?" Dredd demanded.

"He went round a bend," Carroll said. "The cave is really more of a passage. It curls left, then right, and then has a long slope upward."

They all stared into the phantasm-ridden darkness. It seemed the vaporous sprites were all the more active and all the more numerous.

"No, mahn," Bastian muttered shakily, "d'jumbees got him."

Father Carroll sighed. "I mean you no disrespect, Mr. Bastian," he said. "There very well may be evil spirits in this world, jumbees as you call them, but they would not find their way here. This island would repel them."

Bastian defiantly dug his fists into his hips. "Den, whar be d'lad?"

"Hopper?" Carroll called out. "Everything all right in there?"

After a moments pause, there came a voice, distant but resonant. "Right as rain, Guv'nor! You know? I kind of like it in here."

"Ridiculous!" Dredd hissed, charging into the cave's mouth. "You men, follow me."

"Ah, mahn, do I have to?"

Dredd's form seemed to dematerialize in the whirling vapors and the darkness, but his voice emerged with excellent clarity. "Bastian! Do not try my patience!"

For a time, they spoke not a word. Their boots clacked and crackled on the stone floor, snapping off thin bits of limestone and crushing others. Like some great gathering of all the world's will-o'-the-wisps, the colorful, luminous vapors whirled about them all. Bastian seemed the most put off by them, hurdling from one side of the cave to the other just to avoid them. Dredd merely flicked out his free hand as if swatting pesky flies.

After the two bends that were precisely as Carroll had described them, the group caught up to Hopper at a junction of sorts where the cave path began to ascend sharply. "Why have you stopped here?" Dredd demanded.

"Begging your pardon, Guv'nor," he replied. "But it seemed like I should wait."

Dredd shifted on his feet, muttering something under his breath. He took a step toward the incline, turned abruptly, and then paced the cave floor—all the while, waving his torch about like a flag of fire.

"Captain?" Cavendish asked tentatively. "Sir, you all right?"

Dredd didn't answer but continued to pace, now gibbering to himself as if hosting a conversation between three of himself.

"He ain't actin' right," Kilgore muttered, his hand sliding slowly toward the hilt of his cutlass. "What's wrong wid'im?"

Bastian cleared his throat. "It be d'jumb—"

"Don't say it!" Dredd hissed, swinging the torch dangerously close to Bastian's face. "I'm not buying into that supernatural nonsense. But there is something…something wrong here."

"What is it?" Carroll asked.

"I feel something…odd." Dredd scratched at his wiry little patch of beard, a greasy triangular sliver just under his bottom lip. "There is something up there, isn't there, priest?"

"Yes," Carroll replied.

"Something you want me to see?"

Carroll nodded.

"I don't know what your game is," Dredd muttered, drawing his cutlass quick as a striking snake. "But I'll have none of it."

Father Carroll asked, "Are you frightened?"

The last syllable had barely left his lips when Dredd's sword flashed. Carroll felt a sudden, burning sting on the left side of his face, and found a seeping wound where the tip of the cutlass had cut across his cheek.

"A few inches, priest," Dredd snarled. "A few inches and just a bit more pressure to the stroke…and that might have been your head. Mind your words."

Carroll's fingertips smeared the blood in a vain attempt to wipe the wound. Undaunted, he gestured to the rising path. "Will you not go up?"

When no one answered directly, Hopper said, "I'll do it. I'll go take a look-see." No one restrained him, and the lad bounded up the steady incline and out of sight.

A few heartbeats later, he called down, "There's an opening up ahead, I think! And there's light, but it's odd."

"Tell me!" Dredd exclaimed. "What do you see?"

"Not quite there!" Hopper called back. "But the light…oh, the light. It's stunning, it is."

Once again, Dredd paced the cave floor. "What about the light, blast you?"

"It's red, Guv'nor," Hopper called back. "It's red light."

CHAPTER FIFTEEN

IN THE MIDST OF RED LIGHT

"I'll get to the bottom of this," Dredd growled, unsheathing his cutlass once more. "Bastian, Kilgore, Cavendish, you keep an eye on the priest, and watch our flanks for surprises. So help me, Carroll, whatever's up there had better be worth all this trouble."

The priest smiled, but there was no mirth in it. "Oh, it'll be worth the trouble, I'm quite certain. One way…or another."

Dredd set the pace, blasting limestone with each lunging footfall. He clambered up the incline as if he had a score to settle with the mountain itself.

Soon, a reddish glow lit their way, kindling brighter as they climbed. By the time they caught up to Hopper, he was just a silhouette against what seemed a brilliant red sunset blasting its last rays into the cave. Only it wasn't sundown. Or sun up, for that matter. It was still hours before dawn. And yet, the red light persisted.

"What…madness is this?" Dredd whispered.

"No madness at all," Carroll replied. "Go on. See for yourself."

Dredd sneered, muttered something under his breath, and then turned so abruptly that the flame of his torch faltered. He charged by Hopper and kept climbing. The lad followed quickly along, and the others gave chase.

The light was a rich, warm crimson and seemed to fill Dredd's field of vision. Suddenly, the cave walls fell away, and he stepped out onto a wide shelf of stone. It was a vast cliff, looking out over a valley hidden from all who might have searched from the cove where they'd moored *The Red Corsair*. Dredd dropped his sword, dropped his torch, and slowly moved out upon the limestone balcony.

Hopper saw Captain Dredd, the cliff, the red light. More brilliant than before, scarlet rays shone from across the valley and more radiated up from down below. And, while ten thousand diamonds still winked and blinked in the black velvet sky above, Hopper found himself drawn, almost hypnotically, to the red light, to the edge of the cliff. There, just a few steps from a perilous fall, he stopped. At last, he understood the source of the ethereal red light.

Jewels.

The red light shone from thousands of dazzling red jewels. *Likely rubies*, Hopper thought. But these, like the gems upon the shore, were gigantic and lit by inner flame. The gems seemed embedded in the cliffs in irregular concentric circles. *It reminds me of something,* Hopper thought but, whatever it was—memory, concept, or recognition— he couldn't fathom it.

Dredd's mouth worked, but no voice came forth. He stood as one stricken. He bathed in the crimson light. And, as he stared, the curling strands of gems seemed to form a pattern. Rows and rows of red jewels waved and whirled toward an intricate eye, like a stunning scarlet hurricane.

Hopper looked away from the red spectacle. Bastian, Kilgore, Cavendish, and Father Carroll had each taken a private vantage on that vast stone shelf. Each seemed captivated by the sight. But none so much as Captain Dredd. The pirate stood so completely still that Hopper couldn't tell if he was breathing.

"Treasures of avarice!" Kilgore exclaimed, startling the others, all but Dredd. "Can it be real? Can there be so many jewels?"

"The priest led us true," Cavendish whispered. "He's led us to the greater treasure."

"Jumbees cahn take me now," Bastian said, "now dat I have seen such an ocean of rubies."

"Is...is that all you see?" Captain Dredd asked, his voice oddly clear of its coarse anger. "The spoils of invasion? A treasure to be pillaged?"

Kilgore swallowed deeply. "But...that's why we're here."

"Surely, you know what this means, Captain Dredd?" Cavendish mumbled, feeling his next words might just be his last. "This—this treasure—is our freedom. We could buy castles and fortresses and islands to build them upon. We could have our own navy to rival any nation on earth. We—"

"You are as shortsighted as you are dimwitted," Dredd hissed, the venom returning to his voice. "But I fear I have been far worse." He blinked, and his eyes moved restlessly. "You...you really cannot see?"

"See what, mahn?" Bastian asked.

"So clear, now," Dredd whispered.

Kilgore spoke, his voice wet with saliva, "I don't see anything but a thousand meals of the finest beef, kegs of beer stacked higher than the walls of Windsor Castle, and all my wishes come true."

Cavendish almost seemed to swoon. "Rubies and rubies and more rubies."

"FOOLS!" Dredd erupted. A tear, so red it might have been blood, trickled from his left eye into a scar just beneath and traced a solitary path down his weathered cheek. Dredd saw the clusters of luminous red jewels, glimmering from a bed of forest greenery, night-veiled in shadow. But, in his mind's eye, he saw something more. It was there, vivid, like a memory made real. "Blind fools."

Hopper looked from face to face, hoping someone might explain. But even Carroll was captivated by Captain Dredd's peculiar mania.

And then, the Captain of *The Red Corsair* said, "Roses."

* * * * * * * * *

A rifle shot took a branch off a tree just a foot above Kaylie's head. Cat and Anne corralled the girl, keeping their own bodies between her and the direction from which the shot had come.

"This is ridiculous," Cat grumbled. "We should have never brought you to shore. I'm taking you back to *The Bruce*."

"With all due respect," Kaylie said, "you'll have to pick me up and throw me over your shoulder if you want me off this island. And, if you try it, I'll kick, scream, and flail the whole way, until you drop me. Then, I'll run back."

Cat shook his head. "Stubborn girl," he quipped. "Reminds me so much of someone else I know."

Anne swatted Cat's shoulder.

He winced. "Not *that* shoulder next time, if you please."

"Shoulder's least 'a yer worries," Red Eye said. "If we stay here much longer, a bullet's sure to find ye."

Anne nodded emphatically. "Perhaps, we should find a better spot to hide."

"Sounds like a good idea!" Kaylie shouted.

With Cat and Anne flanking on either side, Red Eye led Kaylie behind the lines of clashing sailors. She caught glimpses of silver blades, red bandanas, wide white eyes, sudden bursts of orange fire, and writhing black shadows.

They stumbled down a foothill and hid behind a ridge of limestone so eroded by the wind, sand, and sea that it poked up like a fence.

Kaylie peeked over the stone and saw Captain Dredd's men. There were so many of them coming down the mountain. *It's like a volcano,* thought Kaylie, *except it's not shooting out lava. It's shooting out pirates!*

"Oooh," Anne hissed. "It rots me within to sit and hide while others fight...while Da fights, maybe for his life."

"Thar he is," Red Eye marveled. "The Sea Wolf hunts again!"

"Where?" Anne cried, half-climbing the stone.

Cat pointed. "Near the fallen trees that crisscross the shore. See?"

"Oh, Da," she muttered. "You're outnumbered."

Kaylie watched in helpless horror as Captain Declan Ross locked swords with two of Dredd's men, forcing their blades up high. Then he spun, jabbed a third pirate who'd come rushing up from behind. Without so much as a glance over his shoulder, Ross yanked the sword from the still falling man, dropped to a dangerous crouch, and swept his cutlass in a low, violent arc, carving the legs out from under the first two men. Kaylie winced.

"I can't just sit here," Anne stormed.

"Nor I," Cat replied.

"Go!" Kaylie exclaimed, surprising them both. "Captain Ross and his sailors can really fight, but there are too many. I'll be safe here with Mr. Red Eye."

"I hate to tell ye this, miss," Red Eye said, "but I'll not be hidin' out with ye. I've a score to settle with Tobias Dredd."

"We can't all leave her," Anne said wearily.

"Yes, you can," Kaylie said. "We're far enough from the fighting. Dredd's men can't even see me here."

"You're quite mad, you know that?" Cat said. "One minute, you're threatening to mutiny if we try to take you to the ship. The next, you're telling us to leave you alone on the outskirts of melee."

Kaylie huffed, reaching down into her will for something...anything. Any sign that her Dreamtreader strength was returning, but it wasn't so. Try as she might, she could not will so

96 · WAYNE THOMAS BATSON

much as a feather into existence. "Look," she said, "you don't really know me. I'm not bragging here, but I'm different from other kids my age."

"You can say that again," Anne said.

"I'm smart," Kaylie went on. "I have lots of experience in dangerous situations, and I'm not the sort of kid who needs a babysitter. Now, you three, get out there and fight."

Cat, Anne, and Red Eye exchanged guilty looks.

"I said, go!" Kaylie growled. "It's no longer your choice. Captain Ross needs you out there."

"I won't forget this," Anne said quietly.

"Nor I," Cat said.

"I'll fight in your honor," Red Eye said.

And, one by one, they disappeared around the limestone wall, into the shadows, and into the ever-shifting tempest of musket shots and cutlass strokes.

Void of all Dreamtreading power, defenseless, and alone, Kaylie put her matchless mind to work. For she didn't plan to stay behind the limestone wall either.

CHAPTER SIXTEEN

ROSES AND THORNES

"Roses?" Kilgore coughed. "Captain, thar be no roses in this valley!"

"He's right, mahn," Bastian replied, turning to face Dredd. "No'ting but rubies, mebbe red diamonds, some kind o' gem we've not seen before. Dis be some trick of d'priest."

With each flicker of Dredd's raging torch, the target of his eyes and expression of his features changed. To Kilgore: rage. To Cavendish: contempt. To Bastian: confusion. To Carroll: guilt.

Hopper was glad not to have Dredd's bloodshot gaze fall on him. He backed away from the men, drawing ever closer to the cliff's edge.

"What trick could I play?" Carroll asked, his voice strangely bold. "I'm a priest, not some conjuring magician."

Dredd's eyes continued to scan. "But it was you who brought me to see this place," he whispered.

"Right, right!" Cavendish cackled. "The priest's trying to tug at threads best left alone! There's our future waiting out there! I say we go claim it!" Kilgore nodded emphatically. Bastian edged closer to Dredd.

"You might…be right," Dredd said quietly. His eyes drifted once more past the cliff's edge to the crimson vision. "But, perhaps, this thread is long overdue for a good pull. Perhaps, I've misunderstood…all this time, for I see the roses."

"You're mad, mahn," Bastian said. "Bewitched!"

"I was," Dredd replied, ice in his words. "But…I think I have clarity you sorely lack."

"I've got clarity, all right," Cavendish said, shoving past Bastian. "I know a fortune when I see it. I'll leave you to your roses, but I'm going to climb down into this valley and take me all the jewels I can carry."

"You won't," Dredd said flatly. He lifted his cutlass toward Cavendish. The man drew his own blade, tried to deflect Dredd's blow, but failed. Dredd's cutlass slipped in and out of Cavendish's ribs in a blink. The man reeled backward, scrabbled at the air, and then toppled over the cliff.

"You—you've killed Cavendish!" Kilgore shrieked. He leaped backward, colliding hard with Hopper and then sprinted back toward the tunnel's opening.

Hopper flailed, losing his balance. Dredd swung the torch round and slammed it into Kilgore's upper back. The fire took to the man's jacket and hair. He screeched and fled, knocking Father Carroll flat on his back.

"Ah!" Hopper cried, rocking backward. Dredd dropped his torch, lunged and caught Hopper's wrist.

In that moment, Bastian cursed, charged, and rammed a long knife into Dredd's stomach. Dredd groaned and, still keeping Hopper from going over, weakly raised his cutlass. It was a feeble attempt. Bastian used his bare arm to knock the blade away. Then he stabbed Dredd a second time. A third. The fourth thrust never happened.

Father Carroll sprang across the cliff floor and rammed his shoulder so hard into Bastian's chest that there came an audible cracking of bone. Bastian spun on his heel. Then, eyes bulging and mouth agape, Bastian went backward over the edge.

"Save the lad!" Dredd shouted, groaning with one last effort. He managed to sling Hopper onto safer ground, but the limestone beneath

Dredd's feet cracked and crumbled. Dredd slipped, fell hard to one knee, scrabbled for a handhold, and slowly, inexorably, began to slide.

* * * * * * * * * *

Like shackle and chains, guilt and worry trailed behind Griffin "Cat" Thorne as he sprinted across the sand. No matter his motives, he'd abandoned his post, leaving Kaylie alone on shore with death and murder just a short run away. And, while he knew there'd be no denying Anne her place in this battle, she was the woman he loved and his wife-to-be. Anything could happen out on the shifting sand and in the dusky shadows of an unfamiliar terrain. One flick of the wrist, one misstep, one drop of the guard—and gone.

"Don't start thinking that way!" Anne shouted, just a few strides behind him.

"What way?" he called back.

"You're worrying, aren't you? Afraid something will happen to me or Kaylie or some such thing!"

Cat was flummoxed. He half turned to look over his shoulder and yelled in feigned indignation, "Begone from my mind, woman!"

"Eyes straight ahead, Cat!" she cried out. "Worry about what's ahead, not behind. And remember, I've got your back."

Cat's next breath felt like fire in his lungs. When he exhaled, it was as if he expelled every doubt, every fear, and every indecision. Anne had his back and he would have hers. And together, they would turn the tide of the battle.

Cat set his sights on the closest action. One of Dredd's men, a swarthy fellow with no shirt but enough body hair to qualify as part bear, swayed where he stood over a fallen opponent. The hairy fellow raised a horrendously heavy-looking maul overhead, and prepared to bring it down. But Cat dove, in an instant, lunging across ten feet of sand, and plunging his cutlass into the man's ribs. Cat followed his opponent's plummeting form and drove him straight to the sand.

As he did so, Anne leaped, rolled across Cat's back, and crossed blades with a hooded pirate twice her size. He held a long Scottish claymore in one hand as if it were a cutlass and not a two-fisted blade. In his other hand he had a short boarding axe.

Anne was not foolish enough to keep her distance. He had twice her range. She scraped her cutlass along the claymore's blade and spun outside of his right arm. He tried to rotate his torso to bring that axe around, but it was just too much distance and too little time. Anne's cutlass flicked once, burying the tip into the thick muscle at the man's neck. She gave a twist and a mighty, sawing tug. The fellow's hooded head drooped limply, and he collapsed. But Anne hadn't seen the Spanish pirate ducking out from behind a fat palm. She hadn't seen him lift his flintlock pistol and cock the arm back.

But Cat had seen everything. He stabbed forward, impaling the pirate's hand, pushing his aim far wide of Anne. The gun fired errant and then dropped from the man's hand. Cat gave two quick strokes with his cutlass. The pirate clutched vainly at both bubbling wounds and fell.

Cat and Anne raced on, carving their way across the shoreline to the edge of the trees where a trio of Dredd's men seemed to materialize from thin air. They stepped out of the shadows of the trees. The first man, pear-shaped with rolls of fat that swayed as he moved, wielded some kind of whaling pike with a wicked barbed point on the end. The second man had a pistol in each hand and a dozen more crisscrossing his chest on twin bandoliers. The third man held a machete in one hand and a dripping bottle of rum in the other. They were of such vivid types that Cat couldn't help but think of them as: Tubby, Gunny, and Drunk.

Cat's eyes met Anne's and, without a word, they split. Gunny's first two pistol shots tore hunks of wet palm flesh from the trees where Cat and Anne had been. Cat dove, rolled across a sandy patch, rose, and drove his cutlass for Tubby's midsection. *I can hardly miss,* he'd been thinking, but miss he had. Tubby's spear dashed Cat's blade aside with ease. The big man's reply, a dire thrust, tore through the leather at the waist of Cat's coat and nicked his hip with the tip's jagged barbs.

"You move like a slug!" Tubby blurted, his voice sounding more like an extended belch than actual speech.

Cat's left hand dropped to his side and came up bloody. "You're quite right," he said. "I won't underestimate you again." Cat whipped his cutlass up, spun, and put his entire body into a guillotine-like chop. With a splintering crack, Cat severed the barbed tip from the spear.

"That's not fair!" Tubby croaked. He took the spear in both hands and gave Cat a shove that sent him careening ten feet away into the low foliage.

"Cat, stay down!" Anne yelled.

Cat rose just in time for a pistol shot to tear past his ear. *Oh,* he thought. *That's why.* Cat raced a slow half circle to keep Tubby between himself and Gunny.

"You should have listened!" Anne grumbled.

"Now's not the time!" Cat fired back.

Anne ducked Drunk's machete, slashed at his feet, and lunged toward the stone for better footing. "We may not have a better time!" Anne groused. "And I've been wondering: what shall I do with my name?"

Tubby's spear swooshed over Cat's head, jutted a quick 1-2-3 thrust pattern that had Cat dancing, slipping, and sliding on the sandy ground. "Your...your name?" he coughed.

Anne's cutlass snaked through Drunk's spastic machete defense but met the rum bottle, shattering the glass with a clinking splatter.

"That wuz me last bottle!" Drunk objected.

"My married name, of course!" Anne carped. She parried a machete slash and snapped a thrust close to Drunk's ribs. "I mean, I want to honor you by taking your surname."

"Have you lost your m—ungh!" Tubby's spear shaft struck Cat's jaw. He toppled but recovered in time to avoid the second strike. He lashed out, sticking his cutlass into Tubby's thigh. At the same moment, Gunny's pistol barked again. The shot made a bloody mess of Tubby's left shoulder.

"Watch where you fire those blasted things!" Tubby hissed.

Anne threw a shoulder into Drunk's chest, and sent him staggering backward. "If I go with Anne Elizabeth Thorne, I get to keep my middle name," she said, thinking aloud. "I want to honor my mother, you know? But if I don't keep Ross too, I feel like I'll hurt my Da."

"Anne!" Cat bellowed, striking out to take advantage of Tubby's disorientation. But the big man proved again to be far more nimble and deft than Cat expected. Tubby switched hands with his spear, blocked Cat's thrust, and pushed him back.

"Well?" Anne asked. "What do I do, then? Keep them both? Anne Elizabeth Ross Thorne? But that's so long." She leaped to avoid Drunk's weak attempt to take out her legs.

"Anne, I really don't care what name you use!" Cat snapped. He managed to duck Tubby's errant spear-swipe and finally got the room for an accurate slash. His cutlass carved into the big man's armpit, and that limb went limp.

"What?" Anne blurted. She dropped her guard for just a moment, but that was enough. Drunk's machete clanged off her fist guard and gashed her wrist. Her cutlass fell from her hand. "You don't care?"

Cat spun back the other way and finished Tubby by kicking him so hard that he tumbled head-first into a hump of stone. "I don't care what name," Cat growled, leaping and sprinting to avoid being an easy target for Gunny. "I don't care what name, so long as you'll be my wife!"

"Aww," Anne muttered, her lower lip trembling. She was so distracted that she paid no attention to blood running from her wounded wrist. Worse, she didn't see Drunk hauling back his machete, preparing a ruinous stroke against her.

"Anne!" Cat cried. "Look out!" But, focused on her, Cat hadn't recognized Gunny's movements. He'd drifted toward the tree line, dropped to a crouch, and lifted a long-barreled pistol.

But Anne had seen. "Cat!" she shrieked.

Someone yelled, "Now, mon!"

CHAPTER SEVENTEEN

A STARRY TRAIL TO FOLLOW

Kaylie's mind raced as she stared over the protective limestone wall at the battlefield. The shore had become a twilight battlefield, Dredd's men and Captain Ross's men, grappling, dueling, firing pistols—gaining ground or losing ground. It was strangely beautiful, she thought. The gems lit the sand in muted color. The stars, bright overhead, seemed to mirror the shore. Intermittent sparks kindled at the clash of swords, and pistols discharged blooms of orange and white. Beautiful, but only when she could detach her thoughts from the reality of people being wounded or killed.

It was intricate too, like an oversized chess board with ten times the normal number of pieces—a challenge Kaylie Keaton would normally have welcomed, but this one taxed her thinking. With a glance, she saw the gathering of great stones up the slope from the shore. If she could lever its base, it would send an avalanche of deadly boulders careening down the slope toward the shore. But, of course, such a move would kill as many of Ross's men as it would pirates.

What could she do on the battlefield itself? Short of throwing jewels at the pirates and likely getting trampled, she could see no way through the melee. She wanted to find Hopper and Father Carroll if she could, but where to begin? She didn't know the island. She didn't have a map or a weapon or Dreamtreader powers.

She slumped down against the limestone barricade and felt a great weight upon her heart. *I'm alone, and there's absolutely nothing I can do.* But no sooner had that dark thought slithered into Kaylie's mind, than a flurry of brighter ideas blazed a starry trail of hope for her to follow:

Never alone.

Endurance and victory.

Anchor first; anchor deep.

"Whoa," Kaylie muttered. It was all true, of course. It was all right there. *I'm not alone,* she thought. *God is with me. But, if I hope to see victory, I've got to endure. And that means, I need to drop anchor right now. I need to anchor myself deep...in prayer.*

So, instead of slouching and sulking, Kaylie knelt. And she prayed. She prayed for Hopper, for Father Carroll, for Captain Ross, and for Cat, Anne, and the rest of the crew. She even prayed for Captain Dredd and the crew of *The Red Corsair.*

* * * * * * * * *

Drunk's fearsome machete hung poised in the air, a heartbeat away from a perilous arc toward Anne's neck. Gunny pulled back the hammer of his menacing pistol, leveled the barrel with Cat's chest, and smiled.

Unaware of the more imminent threat to self, Anne and Cat each cried out to warn the other. But someone else spoke nearby, and then, the world erupted in flame.

One second, Gunny was there. The next, a gout of fire tore up from the ground as if a conduit to the center of the earth had opened. The shockwave of the explosion knocked Cat into the forest. His ears rang, but he thought he heard someone shout, "Ho, ho! Boom!"

The explosion rocked Anne back on her heels and, at last, she saw her own danger: the machete slicing through the air toward her. Until it wasn't.

There was a secondary explosion, but this one more of a thunderous bark. Still falling, Anne watched Drunk blown backward clear off his feet and a good fifteen feet into the shaggy foliage beyond.

Blinking and gaping, Anne landed on her back and stared up to see Stede standing beside her, his blunderbuss nicknamed "Thunder Gun," held up against his shoulder. The twin barrels were still smoking.

Stede helped Anne to her feet, and she hugged him. Someone pulled her free. She turned and Cat gathered her into an embrace. Over his shoulder, she saw Jacques St. Pierre, standing a few feet away. He wore a wicked grin and had only one of his three powder barrels left.

"Some advice, mon ami," Jacques St. Pierre said, "you might wish to pick a better time and place to speak of wedding plans, *T'sais?*"

"I'll second that, mon," Stede said, wiping down the flint pan of his blunderbuss. "But c'mon, now. *The Bruce* be needin' us."

"*The Bruce?*" Cat echoed, releasing Anne.

"Capitaine's orders!" St. Pierre replied. "He sent us to find you."

"*The Red Corsair* has hoisted anchor," Stede explained. "Openin' fire upon *d'Bruce*. Captain Ross b'wantin' us aboard to fight back."

"Where's my father?" Anne demanded.

"He and Red Eye be headin' after Dredd himself."

* * * * * * * * *

Cannon fire forced a premature "Amen" from Kaylie. Like a beach prairie dog, she poked her head up from the limestone wall, and saw two ships—*The Red Corsair* and *The Robert Bruce*—exchanging cannon blasts. It was like watching two thunderstorms fight.

The clash of the battle on shore called her attention back. Kaylie watched as several of Captain Ross's sailors were taken down. Without thinking, she raced toward the tree line, and wove in and out of the trees, skirting the fighting. She stumbled onto a path that seemed to snake its way up one of the island's tallest peaks. She didn't know why, but she felt drawn to that path, and she started to run up the slope when a voice rose above the fighting.

"Cease fire, men of *The Red Corsair*!" the voice commanded. "Put down those rifles and put those swords away!"

The voice was deep and bold and full of power.

Most of the pirates lowered their weapons.

Captain Ross's men did too.

But who could command them like that? Kaylie wondered. Then she heard a pistol shot, and she saw a tall pirate coming down the mountain. He wore a long coat and was all in black.

CHAPTER EIGHTEEN

THE FEAR OF GOD

Cat swung *The Robert Bruce's* wheel round to port, praying silently to recapture the gusty trade wind he needed. "Come on," he hissed at the stormy dawn sky. "Come on!"

"It's coming!" Anne assured, hovering at his shoulder. "It's whipping at the rigging and shrouds. Just a little more to port and we'll catch!"

A voice from above burst through the wind. "*The Corsair's* closing!" Nock cried out.

"Dey be comin' about, mon!" Stede agreed. "If d'wind not kind, we be needin' to force 'dem off target."

"Port cannons!" Cat bellowed. "Fire!"

But, aside from the howling wind, there came no answer from *The Bruce's* gunnery.

"It's d'wind, mon!" Stede said.

"Where's Red Eye?" Cat groused.

"On d'isle!"

"I'll go," Anne said. No sooner had she turned to the bridge stair than the square-rigged sails snapped to full, and the ship wrenched hard to port. Anne fell to a knee and skidded into the stair rail.

At the same time, there came a strange crackling overhead, followed by a series of distant thunderclaps. Anne crumpled even further, throwing up her arms to guard the back of her head.

The Red Corsair's cannons had disgorged, but they weren't the mast-cracking heavyweight shots, not 32 or 42 pounders, nor the newest 67 pound carronade ship-killers. No, these were something different. The strange crackling was followed by searing heat. Anne risked a look, saw flames crawling up the bunt lines and shrouds of the foremast. Another hungry fire raged on the bowsprit. Still another was eating a ragged, charred hole in the fore topsail. "Heaven help us," Anne muttered. "They're not trying to cripple us. They're trying to burn us alive!"

She righted herself quickly, lunging across the deck and racing to the portside cannoneers. She wove behind the crews, yelling, "The captain ordered you to fire! Fire, now!"

A stout man came running to Anne's side. He wore a gray vest over a white shirt, dark leather breeches, and heavy black boots. He had a broad face, festooned with a stubbly square jaw, a prominent wide nose, and the cleverest thin slits of brown eyes Anne had ever seen.

"Who are you?" Anne demanded.

"McDonald, Miss Anne," he replied with a curt bow. "Clinton McDonald. Backup master gunner."

That explains why I've never seen you, Anne thought. Red Eye doesn't give up his charge lightly. "Look, McDonald, you need to position yourself much closer to the bridge. You missed the command to fire!"

"What?" McDonald gave a most wretched look. "I knew it! Portside, right? What pattern?"

"Pattern?" Anne blanked. Her mind raced. Then, she just blurted, "Fear of God pattern, Mister McDonald! Give them the fear of God."

"Aye, sir!" McDonald barked. Then, he stammered, "I mean...aye, Ma'am!"

Anne barely heard him. She'd spun on her heel and sprinted for the bridge. She'd reached the top step when *The Robert Bruce's* entire port side erupted in a deafening roar of fire and smoke.

Anne had heard *The Bruce* open up before, many times, but there was no getting used to that kind of thunderous calamity. It shook her to the bone, and she trembled as she went to Cat's side.

Cat didn't take his hands from the wheel, but he turned and looked upon her with gratitude, admiration, and adoration.

"Let's see how dem devils handled 'dat—" Stede never finished that thought. "Oh! Oh, mon."

In the dawn twilight, they all saw the impact of *The Bruce's* fearsome salvo. How many of the forty port cannon had McDonald fired at once? Anne didn't know. But it looked as if at least twenty had struck *The Red Corsair*. The low slung vessel buckled amidships. Two of its masts, with their angular, shark fin sails, came crashing inward. Flames sprang up like wounds of fire, and one explosion in particular tore a chunk out of the hull near the bowsprit.

"Fear of God," Anne whispered.

"What?" Cat asked.

"Nevermind."

"White flags!" Nock yelled from the crow's nest high on the main mast.

"Look 'dere!" Stede pointed.

The black flag of *The Red Corsair*, the skull and crossed roses, dropped like a stone. Flags of soiled white rose in its place and on the rigging of any mast or spar still standing.

"It's over," Anne whispered. "We've won."

"The battle," Cat said, taking her hand in his. "But the war will be decided on shore."

* * * * * * * *

"Defy me at your peril!" shouted the man, careening down the mountain path. His eyes were wide, his expression dire, and he held a bloody hand to his ribs. "Captain Tobias Dredd commands you!"

Kaylie felt a chill. *Captain Dredd? He ordered the cease fire?*

The tall pirate captain fired a pistol in the air. He tossed it aside, took another from his bandolier and fired it as well. Pistol after pistol, some fourteen shots, Dredd fired, all the while, he demanded, "HEAR ME! Put down your arms! Do not fire another shot!"

Dredd flung away his last pistol, drew his cutlass, and perched himself upon a limestone promontory that overlooked the northern curl of the shore. He stood like a fierce statue, but with a voice like thunder at sea. Soon, the clamor of his pirates and Captain Ross's sailors clashing diminished to nothing, and a crowd gathered below him.

A stooping pirate with slanted eyebrows, pointy ears, and a smoking scalp appeared from another mountain path. Like a spider, he climbed up the hill to Captain Dredd. "This is poor timing," the man said. "Captain Dredd, we have our enemy in the palm of our hand. Will you not discard your madness and lead us to victory!"

Captain Dredd glared at the pirate. "Mr. Kilgore," he said, "you dare question my leadership?"

Kilgore bent lower, like a dog that had been swatted.

"Victory, you say?" Dredd boomed. "Look out to sea. *The Red Corsair* is ruined! *The Robert Bruce* has spoken and left us without reply. But even if it had not been so, I would command surrender!"

Captain Dredd looked over the silent crowd. "I climbed this mountain on an island of riches, searching for even greater riches," he said. "And...I have found them."

CHAPTER NINETEEN

BROKEN THINGS

The crowd rumbled with excitement.

Kaylie cringed. *Where is Hopper?* she wondered. *Is he still on Captain Dredd's ship?* She gasped. The Bruce *just pummeled* The Red Corsair*! If Hopper was aboard...*

"Hear me!" Captain Dredd shouted from the outcropping of pale stone. "The treasure I speak of...it is not the collection of jewels scattered across this island."

It seemed to Kaylie as if a great wall of wind had suddenly swept away all the sound except for Captain Dredd's voice. Only Kilgore moved, squirming to and fro like a pinned snake upon a wedge of limestone just below Dredd.

"I was sure God hated me," Captain Dredd explained. He held up his blood-smeared hand and pointed accusingly at the sky. "After all, God gouged my mother from my life, set me on a path of bloodshed and bitter victories. I blamed God...and I hated Him. But I was wrong."

"Who cares about God?" Kilgore asked, his hand trembling close to the hilt of his cutlass. "When we can have a king's hoard of jewels?"

Many of the pirates in the crowd murmured agreement.

"We came here to get rich!" someone shouted.

"Yeah!" a different pirate crowed. "Sick and tired of living hand-to-mouth!"

"Jewels, jewels!" answered a third man. "Jewels enough for all!"

"Can you take jewels with you beyond the grave?" Dredd asked. He hesitated a moment, glancing down at his seeping gut wounds. "But…I understand the blindness. The jewels are a glittering prize, a soft-spoken promise of better days ahead. I too shared this blind dream. But now, I see with greater clarity. All the jewels and gold in the world cannot give you what they seem to promise."

"This is foolishness!" one man yelled.

"You're mad!"

"No!" Dredd shouted, and then, he doubled over in a fit of wet coughing. When he straightened, blood glistened in one corner of his mouth. "I was mad, before. I am sane, now, lads. More sane than I've ever been. God did not take my mother from me. God brought my mother to her home. Her true home."

"You speak of heaven," Kilgore said, slowly loosening the cutlass from its sheath. "But there is no heaven for the likes of us. We have lived evil lives."

"Yes," Dredd said. "Yes, we have. There are black stains of mayhem and murder upon each of us. Upon me more than any of you, for I led most of you into lives of atrocity and cheered on your violence."

"There is naught but hell for us!" Kilgore growled. "Naught but hell."

Clamor broke out in the crowd. There was shouting, and a few swords met.

Someone took hold of Kaylie's shoulder. She spun around to find Captain Ross, Mister Stede, and Jacques St. Pierre standing in the twilight, among the slender trees behind her.

"Come, Kaylie," Ross whispered. "We've got to get you away from here."

"Not now," Kaylie argued. "Please, not now. I need to hear this."

Ross looked out to the crowd. "Things are going to go badly, I fear. We cannot delay much longer."

"Hell?" Dredd shouted, his voice strained. "Hell is what we all deserved, but Father Carroll tells me that we, yes—even such as we—might yet be saved. Do you know why the priest brought us here? It wasn't fear of death, I can tell you. Nay! He wanted us to see this island. He wanted us to see one of the few wonders of this world not besmirched by man. Have you seen? Have you opened your eyes to this, this wondrous place?"

If anything the crowd became more agitated. The murmur became an angry buzz.

"Kaylie," Ross whispered. "I think we should get you out—"

"Answer me this, then!" Dredd shouted above the clamor. "How could it be that this island holds something just for me? Father Carroll took me up to that peak. Beyond it is a valley full of red jewels, but not some random arrangement, for I saw roses! Roses sent to me from my mother...roses from heaven!"

The crowd began to undulate like a storm-tossed sea. Kaylie took hold of Captain Ross's sleeve and asked, "What does he mean, 'roses from heaven?'"

Captain Ross said, "I am not certain, Kaylie. But I do know that Captain Dredd left a rose on every ship he defeated. It was to honor his dead mother."

Suddenly, Kilgore raised his cutlass and pointed it at Captain Dredd. "'Roses from heaven, you say?'" Kilgore asked. "The priest has put you under a spell, if you think you saw roses. I was there, Dredd! I saw no such thing as that."

Dredd's cutlass flashed about, leveling the point to match Kilgore's own. "I saw the roses," he said, "just as clearly as I see you now."

"What of them?" Kilgore shrieked. "Roses in jewels or just jewels? What does it matter? What, then, would you have us all do?"

"Turn!" Captain Dredd shouted. "Turn from our path! Stop fighting over jewels! Listen to Father Carroll—just hear him out. He has words of life!"

"Turn?" Kilgore said. "Just like that? But we won't live. We will all be hung!"

"Nay," Captain Dredd said. "Only me."

"How?" Kilgore asked.

Captain Dredd answered, "I am the one Captain Ross here wants." Dredd pointed his sword toward Captain Ross and said, "If I turn myself in, will you grant pardon to my crew?"

Captain Ross said nothing. To Kaylie, he seemed frozen. "Captain Ross?" she asked.

He seemed to wake up. "That is a lot of pardons," Captain Ross said. "But if your men leave the jewels of this rare island alone, if they abandon violence against my crew, and if you turn yourself in, we will pardon them."

"Agreed," said Captain Dredd.

"Not agreed!" Kilgore shouted. "Men, pirates we be! Listen, all you who are true to *The Red Corsair*! Your captain has lost his nerve! And worse, he killed his own men. I saw him slay Cavendish and Bastian in cold blood! He's not fit to command, I tell you! Fight under me! Kill Dredd, kill Captain Ross, and kill anyone else who stands between you and the jewels that are rightfully yours!"

* * * * * * * *

Father Carroll and Hopper stumbled down the mountain path just in time to see Kilgore lock swords with Dredd on the stone promontory. At its base, pirates and sailors teemed, engaging in such a violent melee that it was impossible to tell who was on whose side.

"I was afraid this would happen," Father Carroll said. "Dredd meant well, I think, but I should never have let him run off. Come lad!"

Hopper raced after the priest and frantically scanned the combatants. For all he knew, Kaylie might be in the middle of it all. But he wouldn't let himself despair. Kaylie was no lightweight. She had guts and faith and some pretty powerful allies.

"Stop!" Father Carroll yelled. "Tobias, you can't win them this way!" He instantly regretted his words, for Dredd looked up, taking his eyes off Kilgore. The scoundrel slid his cutlass off Dredd's block and jabbed the blade into his shoulder.

"Gah!" Dredd yelled, spinning away from Kilgore. He tumbled down the side of the rock formation and into the crowd. Kilgore leaped down the other side and was lost in the fighting.

Father Carroll had no sword, no dagger, no pistol, but he raced into the melee. But Hopper was faster. He's spent many years as a beggar, weaving in and out of crowded streets, his slight frame bending and twisting eel-like to avoid notice…or capture.

He found Captain Dredd, his back to the foot of the pale stone outcropping. Hopper grabbed the man's arm. "Get up! Get up!" Hopper urged. "Kilgore's coming!"

Father Carroll was there a moment later. "What? Hopper? You should have—never mind. Here, Dredd, can you stand?"

"I can manage," Captain Dredd said angrily. He stood up and said, "That traitor Kilgore didn't wound me deep."

"Glad to hear it," Father Carroll said.

"I'm afraid Bastian's knife did more damage," Dredd muttered as he rose. "Ah, Carroll, I don't know how this will end."

"What do you mean?" the priest asked.

"The roses, roses made of ruby jewels," Dredd said hoarsely. "I cannot but think they were left—that God left them—for me to discover. He showed me...these roses. He knows my sorrow."

"So He does, Tobias," Father Carroll said. "He does."

Dredd coughed, and more blood dribbled over his bottom lip. He reached out and gripped Father Carroll's forearm. "But...what good is it?" Dredd asked, his voice reedy and thin. "I am a man of changed mind, but these stomach wounds...are lethal. I am dying. I will never be able to right my wrongs. I'll never be able to do enough good to...overcome all the evil I've done."

"That's easy," Hopper said. "Begging your pardon, Guv'nor. But we're all broken things. We can't work off our sins, so to speak."

Father Carroll nodded. "The lad's right."

"Is there no hope then?" Dredd asked.

Father Carroll looked about. Even in the cleft beneath that limestone formation, the ongoing violence was vividly clear around them. It seemed the most peculiar place for a priest, a pirate captain, and a bald boy to have a theological discussion. At last, with a self-conscious laugh, he said, "Tobias Dredd, your evils, my evils—we cannot wash them clean ourselves, but it is for precisely that reason that God offers us a way."

"Tell me!" Dredd wheezed. "Tell me before it is too late."

"Christ crucified," Carroll replied, steel in his voice. "Hammer and nail, a cross drenched with blood, but Jesus bore it willingly. It was the weight and atrocity of all our sins and the world's besides. But Christ bore it and beat it so that we might live. Believe, Tobias Dredd. That is all Christ asks. Believe."

No hush fell upon the shore. The fighting raged on. But Hopper watched something change in Captain Dredd's expression. Grime, sweat, blood, and tears mingled with ferocity and pain...but there was no longer even so much as a hint of fear.

Captain Dredd looked down, found his cutlass blade a few feet away. Then, without a word to Hopper or to Father Carroll, Dredd raced into the battle, shouting as he ran: "Men loyal to their captain: rally to me! We fight for more than treasure!"

Kilgore and a host of pirates from *The Red Corsair* gave chase, but then, the battlefield changed. Many pirates pulled away and ran to Captain Dredd's aid. Declan Ross and his crew joined the fray, crashing across the sand like a vast rogue wave. Kilgore might still have had a larger force of fighting men, but now, he had Captain Dredd's forces in front and Declan Ross's men behind. And the vice was closing.

"Come, Hopper," Carroll said. "You don't belong in the middle of this." He led Hopper across a hilly ridge, trying to stay away from the fighting, and then, they ran straight into Kaylie.

"Hopper?"

"Kaylie?"

A piece of the ridge gave way. Kaylie slid first. Hopper grabbed her hand but slid as well. They kicked up glowing jewels as they slid twenty feet down, tumbling into the writhing combatants of the fighting on shore.

Carroll went stumbling down the bank and yelled to them, "Stay there and stay down! I'm coming to you!"

Hopper and Kaylie ducked down, but suddenly, Kilgore was there. He snarled at Hopper and Kaylie, raised his bloodied sword and attacked.

Hopper darted in front of Kaylie and used his body to shield her.

"Hopper!" Kaylie shouted. "No!"

Hopper saw Father Carroll sprinting towards them, but knew the priest couldn't get there in time. Kilgore's sharp blade came crashing down. Kaylie screamed.

At that moment, so many things happened. It seemed as if time slowed. It was like watching a man in deep sleep exhale...and then waiting an eternity to see if he would inhale another breath.

A black shape dove in front of Hopper and Kaylie, and Kilgore's sword struck another blade. Kaylie yanked Hopper backward and they both fell.

When they looked up, they couldn't believe their eyes. It was Captain Dredd. He had lunged in front of Hopper and Kaylie to protect them.

Dredd blocked Kilgore's sword. Kilgore, his scalp still smoking, hacked and jabbed and thrust his blade, but he couldn't get through Dredd's superior sword craft. Dredd whipped his blade to the side and back, and then, drove a slicing slash across the fingers of Kilgore's sword hand. He screeched, and the sword flew into the air.

Hopper thought Kilgore was finished but, with his bloody hand, the scoundrel dug into to his belt. He pulled a small black pistol and fired at Captain Dredd's chest. Dredd fell to his back, and his sword clanged out of his hand.

Suddenly, Declan Ross was there. With a savage, blurred stroke, he lopped off Kilgore's gun hand at the wrist. Kilgore went into a frantic, seething, screaming madness. With his one good hand, he went back to his belt and found the handle of a second pistol. Then, he found Declan Ross's sword, plunged deep between his ribs. Kilgore's eyes flickering, he slid off of Ross's sword and slumped to the ground. Gasping and panting, Kilgore's head jerked left and right. He seemed to be searching for something.

Then, his eyes locked onto a large white gem that lay, partially buried in sand, just out of reach. With the stump of his arm flopping uselessly in the direction of the jewel, Kilgore's eyes closed.

"That won't save you," Father Carroll said. "But I know what will." The priest knelt by Kilgore's side and whispered into his ear. But Kilgore didn't stir. He didn't breathe again.

Kaylie and Hopper ran to Captain Dredd's side. "Captain Dredd?" Hopper asked. The pirate's eyes were closed and he looked very old and startlingly pale.

"Captain Dredd?" Hopper repeated.

"Aye, lad," Captain Dredd whispered, his eyelids parting slowly. "I…I'm still here, but I fear not for long."

"You dove in front of us," Hopper said. "Why…why would you do that?"

Captain Dredd laughed quietly but frowned in pain. "Ah," Captain Dredd said, "maybe yesterday, I wouldn't have. But today, I am something new. Besides, isn't that what your Jesus did?"

"He's your Jesus too," Father Carroll said.

Captain Dredd smiled. Wrinkles of tension that had bunched in the center of his forehead, above the bridge of his nose, and around his eyes melted away. His next breath came in a long, glad sigh.

"Alas, I am here too late!" Captain Ross said. "Kilgore's few living pirates have dropped their swords. The battle is won, but it seems, we've lost much also."

"Please," Captain Dredd whispered, his eyes roaming from Father Carroll to Ross and the others. "I would see the roses once more. Could you…take me there?"

Captain Declan Ross gathered a few of his sailors. With Father Carroll leading the way, they carried Captain Dredd back up the mountain, and through the cave. They laid him down on the ledge.

Captain Dredd's eyes were open and clear but glimmering with tears. He stared down at the valley. He saw no gems there, only roses. Their red light covered him like a blanket, and he took his last breath.

CHAPTER TWENTY

OF BRIDES, BRITS, AND BRIGANTINES

Captain Declan Ross stood on the gently rolling deck but seemed anything but at peace. He turned a fierce glare upon Anne and Cat. "You allowed the secondary crew of *The Red Corsair*, a crew without the leadership of any seasoned captain, much less Tobias Dredd, to do this much damage to *The Robert Bruce*?"

"Their use of incendiary shells was unexpected," Cat replied, "as was the *Corsair's* approach from the north side of the island."

"You should be proud of Cat," Anne said, "not punitive. He maneuvered the ship in a fickle wind and managed to cripple the *Corsair* into surrender."

"We didn't lose a single man, sir," Cat added.

Ross clasped his hands behind his back and paced the deck. "For that, I am grateful," he said. "Still, the damage to *The Bruce* was extensive."

Cat nodded. "I plan to help with rep—"

Ross interrupted, holding up a hand. "You understand, the cost of repairs is coming out of your wedding present."

Cat and Anne frowned at each other and turned to Captain Ross just in time to catch his mischievous wink.

Anne smacked her father's shoulder. "You! You…scoundrel!"

Declan Ross laughed heartily, a ringing merry-sounding guffaw that had most of the nearby crew halting in place to watch and listen. "In earnest," Ross said, "Cat and Anne, I couldn't be more proud of how you handled yourselves on the island and especially in charge of *The Bruce*. Tobias Dredd had no such thing as second-rate sailors. His men were handpicked, experienced, and ruthless. If not for your command and the skill of your crew, I suspect that fire and water would yet be vying to consume *The Bruce* right now."

"Thank you, sir."

"Thank you, Da."

"But as it is," Ross went on, "the ship's in no shape for a proper wedding, and repairs must be made. It just wouldn't do for a brides-maid to trip over a piece of wreckage and plummet down into the hold. Fortunately, Father Carroll suggested a solution for both of our concerns. He knows of a guild of talented shipwrights on the north shore of New Zealand, missionaries and tribal peoples alike. They do good work, he says."

"But what about our wedding?" Anne asked, a hint of a frown forming upon her lips. "New Zealand?"

"No, that's the best part," Ross replied. "It seems there's a beautiful farm village there that would be an astonishingly excellent location for your wedding and the celebration to follow. The perfect place for a party, Carroll tells me, even if it's a bit unexpected."

"But can we still get there in time?" Anne asked. "In time for Christmas? You know how desperately I wanted a Christmas wedding."

Ross nodded. "With the favorable winds we're enjoying now, we could likely make the north shore of New Zealand in a week. We'll likely drop anchor on Christmas Eve."

* * * * * * * * *

In Captain Ross's cabin, during the wee hours of the watch, Father Carroll sipped at a snifter of brandy and said, "You let them go after all?"

"Those who followed Dredd," Captain Ross said, "after his—change of heart—those who fought to protect the island and its real treasure. I suspect those men are much changed by all we've seen."

"We all are," said Carroll.

Declan Ross raised his glass in response. "How strong is the God who could change the heart of a man so wicked as Tobias Dredd?"

"Jeremiah 32:27."

"What?" Ross asked.

"From the Old Testament," Father Carroll explained. "'I am the Lord, the God of all mankind. Is anything too difficult for me?'"

Ross laughed thoughtfully.

Father Carroll stared out through the aft windows and saw stars glimmering over the endless black of the South Pacific. "What of the others?" he asked. "Dredd's men who fought against us to the end?"

"Down in the brig," Ross replied.

"What'll become of them?"

"They'll have a very long journey," Ross said. "Need to answer for their crimes. Those that don't hang will spend the rest of their lives imprisoned in Brimstone Hill Fortress in St. Kitts, like as not."

"I wonder, Captain," Carroll said, "would it trouble you if I went to speak to those men in the brig, from time to time, that is?"

"As often as you like," Ross said. "Nothing like a captive audience, eh?"

"Something like that," Carroll replied.

After a heavy silence, Ross asked, "And what of the Isle of Stars? Will the Brethren keep it secret, do you think?"

Father Carroll closed his eyes and sighed. "As a member of the Brethren, I have never once doubted our charge to protect the precious relics and wonders of Almighty God. But I confess this to you, Declan Ross: having seen the impact of the Isle of Stars on Tobias Dredd, I find myself troubled to think that so very few will ever see those glimmering shores."

* * * * * * * * *

On the morning of December 24th, the rising sun set fire to the South Pacific as *The Robert Bruce* made harbor just off of New Zealand's north shore.

Kaylie Keaton stood with Hopper at the port rail and said, "It's beautiful!"

Hopper sighed. "White shores," he whispered, "and then, a far green country. It's almost like…another world."

There was something so idyllic, so wrenchingly fair that she had to turn away. At Hopper's mention of another world, an ache began to throb within her. She was still far from home and had no idea how to return.

"There are other ships moored," Hopper muttered. "Coming into view just now, on the other side of the harbor. So many other ships. Wait, those are British flags!"

* * * * * * * * *

"FATHER!" Anne growled, throwing open his cabin door.

"Is it too much to ask for a knock?"

Anne ignored his question. "You planned this all along! You planned for the wedding to be here in New Zealand. Brandon Blake and Dolphin are here. Half the British Navy is here! That's no accident."

"Sharp as ever, darling daughter," Ross replied coyly. "Wait 'til you see the party grounds. There's a deep green vale set with thirty hand-carved tables and seating for hundreds. Oh, and there's this mighty tree...a great broadleaved thing overhanging the wedding table. We've festooned it with ribbons, garlands, and hanging candles. You've never seen the like."

Anne fell into her father's arms and hugged him so hard that he coughed. "You've not lost your pirate mischief," she whispered, "and for that, I am so grateful."

* * * * * * * *

"Do you, Anne Ross, take this man to be your lawfully wedded husband?" Father Carroll asked. He, Anne, and Cat stood on a heavily garlanded platform beneath the proud tree of which her father had spoken. They were flanked, on one side, by Declan Ross, Stede, and many of *The Bruce's* senior crew. On the other side, stood Admiral Brandon Blake and his wife Dolphin, a half dozen British Navy Captains, Hopper, and Kaylie.

Anne stared fiercely into Cat's eyes. "I do," she declared.

"And do you, Griffin Thorne, take this woman to be your lawfully wedded wife?"

Cat grinned. "I most heartily do."

"Rings, please?" Father Carroll said, nodding to Kaylie and Hopper. Kaylie placed a silver ring in Anne's palm. Hopper gave the other ring to Cat.

"No ring of silver," said Father Carroll, "no priceless jewel could come close to recognizing how precious you both are to God. So, with Christ's words, I impress upon you both, 'Do not worry about your life, what you will eat or what you will wear. Your Heavenly Father knows you need these things.' He will provide for you."

Father Carroll nodded. Cat and Anne took turns placing a wedding ring upon the other's finger.

"In the sight of God and all these witnesses," Father Carroll declared aloud. "I now pronounce you husband and wife. You may kiss the bride!"

Kaylie blushed. Hopper did too, the red washing over his scalp, making him look a bit more like a peach than usual.

At the kiss, a long cheer rose. Musicians struck up the wedding recessional. Father Carroll cried out, "I present to you Mr. and Mrs. Griffin Thorne!"

Cat and Anne leaped together from the platform and were engulfed by the crowd. Kaylie blinked back tears but then, surprising herself, was overcome by the most extraordinary yawn.

* * * * * * * * *

The wedding feast was in full swing when Declan Ross handed Cat and Anne a rolled piece of parchment. "Go on," he said. "Open it."

Cat and Anne exchanged cautious glances. Together, they unrolled the parchment…and gasped.

"These are plans," Cat muttered.

"It's a brigantine," Anne said.

"Not just any brigantine," Ross explained. "It's your brigantine or…at least it will be when Ramiro de Ferro Goncalo completes it this spring. It's from the crew of *The Bruce*. We commissioned its design for you. It'll be your wedding present."

* * * * * * * *

Stede drew near to Declan Ross, pointed, and said, "I don't understand it, mon. Look at Red Eye over dere! Here we be in the middle of a mos' beautiful ting, and da fool mon looks like he been half drowned in vinegar!"

"He's sulking," Ross explained. "He wanted the chance to settle an old score with Tobias Dredd, but old Dredd went and died before Red Eye even made an attempt."

"What a foolish mon," Stede said. "You know what he need, mon? He be needin' a woman."

Stede started to leave, but Ross grabbed his arm. "Wait," he said. "Watch."

Just then, at Red Eye's table, Clint McDonald appeared. On his arm, was a vision of beauty. She had lush brown hair, streaked through with sun-brightened hues. Her glad eyes glimmered, and she smiled demurely as Clint introduced her to Red Eye.

"That's his sister," Ross explained to Stede. "Lucy McDonald. She's a friend of Dolphin Blake's and, according to Clint, has always had an interest in our Red Eye."

Stede let out a great belly laugh. "I'd say d'feelin' be mutual, mon!"

They laughed heartily as Red Eye stood up from the table so fast that he knocked over his chair.

* * * * * * * *

Kaylie had wandered back over to the wedding table. She was tired. Exhausted, really. And, while she thought it a rather rude thing to do, she rested her head on her hands and arms upon the table.

She was awakened from a light doze when Brandon Blake brushed behind her and sat next to Declan Ross.

"I wonder," Blake said, "would you have any interest in sailing to America?"

"America?" Ross blurted. "Whatever for?"

"*The Queen Anne's Revenge*," Blake replied.

Ross laughed. "What on earth is that?"

"No laughing matter, I'm afraid," Blake replied. "It's a pirate frigate, stealthy and fast, and causing no small amount of havoc off America's east coast."

Ross sighed. "You've other seasoned hunters," he said. "I should like a bit of rest, I think."

"Before you say no," Blake went on, "know that you've met the captain of *The Queen Anne's Revenge*. He goes by the name Blackbeard."

"Blackbeard?" Ross snorted. "Never heard of him."

"Not by that name," Blake explained. "But he once served under Bartholomew Thorne. His real name is Edward Teach."

Kaylie heard the sound of a knife clattering on a plate, but nothing more.

EPILOGUE

In his cabin aboard *The Queen Anne's Revenge*, Edward Teach faced a round, grease-smeared mirror and sneered. He grimaced. Then, he scowled. "No, not quite menacing enough," he muttered. "Not for Blackbeard."

Meowr.

Teach glanced to his roll top desk and found a green-eyed tabby cat staring back at him expectantly. Teach glowered briefly at the beast and went back to his reflection. He took a small fork-like comb from the shelf beneath the mirror and set to working at his ever-thickening beard. *Funny,* he thought, *I hadn't so much as a whisker 'til I hit 26 years of age, and now, at 32, the beard's a thick and wiry jungle of black, spreading by the day.*

With the ship moored off the Carolinas' barrier islands, the summer air could hardly be more humid, and his dampened beard hung like sable Spanish moss all the way down to his belt. The beard climbed too, much like a vine. Over time, its tendrils crawled up from his mouth, over his cheekbones, and threatened even now to reach his eyes. Such a beard was one in a thousand—perhaps, one in a million—and it was as much Teach's trademark as it was his piratical name.

Teach twisted the comb to pull wiry strands of black this way and that until they formed a kind of wild animal's mask. He frowned and grinned maniacally, calling upon his facial muscles to form the most demonic scowl.

Better, he thought. *Showing the whites of my eyes...I'll have to remember—*

"What in blazes?" Teach blurted. He looked down to find a purring Russian Blue gliding in and around his boots. "Maria!" he shouted at his half open cabin door. "Come feed yer cats! They be driving me mad!"

No answer. Teach lifted his foot and gave the cat a harmless but firm shove.

The Russian Blue replied with *Rowr!*

Teach scanned his cabin. There was a very orange British shorthair perched on the windowsill, a tubby Himalayan pawing at something behind a crate, a lanky Burmese gray strolling leisurely across a heavy chest, and even a mischievous Havana Brown chasing its tail upon his chart table.

"Maria!" he boomed, giving his full-on surrender-your-vessel voice. "Come feed your blasted cats! Bah, why do I allow you to have these infernal creatures aboard my ship?"

When, again, there was no response, Teach was temped to draw his cutlass and be done with the wretched little scavengers. But, for the moment, he held his temper in check, deciding instead to search for his errant serving wench.

Quick glances up on the main deck and then down in the holds were fruitless, but when Teach heard the shouting from the galley, he knew he'd found her at last. He burst through its swinging door and found the chamber packed, his crew cheering and jeering some sort of heated competition. *Young Maria,* Teach thought as he pushed through the men. *Showing off...as usual.*

He found raven-haired Maria locked in a tense arm wrestling match with Oliver Howell, the ship's cook. Howell grunted and hissed, but Maria was silent. Her bright blue eyes smoldered, staring daggers at her much older opponent.

"Oh, stop making him suffer!" Teach growled. "Get it over with!"

Oliver's face went sheet-white. Maria's impish smile widened. She turned her shoulders and wrenched her right hand, driving her opponent's knuckles hard onto the tabletop.

Ketch's axe, but she's strong! Teach thought. *And just fourteen.*

Maria released her opponent's hand, turned, and beamed up at Teach. It was the same smile that had forced him to haul her up out of the water just off the Spanish coast, six years back. There had been a frightful cannon battle between nine pirate vessels. *The Queen Anne's Revenge* was one of only three ships left seaworthy. Under the blazing Mediterranean sun, Teach had combed the wreckage, looking for anything of value, when he came across then nine-year-old Maria, clinging with one arm to a listing section of a less fortunate ship's hull. In the other arm, she cradled a sopping wet kitten.

"Please, sir," was all Maria had said. The bright sun had gleamed in her eyes, and Teach had thrown her a line. He'd kept her on as a serving wench, though, in truth, he doted upon her like a daughter. She was the one good and pure thing left in his life.

"Maria," he growled, "get ye down to my cabin and feed those vermin you call pets!"

The girl leaped up from her chair, curtseyed to Teach, and scurried away.

"As for you," Teach said, turning his scowl onto Oliver Howell, "get ye back to the kitchen. Lift some sacks of flour, knead some dough, and tenderize some meat—anything to put some strength in those wiry arms!"

Howell disappeared into the laughing, jostling crowd. Then, Teach felt a presence behind him.

"Captain, sir?" Martin Jones, Teach's bug-eyed lookout, said. "There's another merchant comin' to yield its bounty."

"Another?" Teach echoed with a laugh. "It's almost too easy. Should have thought of a blockade such as this years ago."

"Only works because of the fear," Martin observed. "They've all heard the tales, and they's a'feared to run from ye."

"So they'd rather surrender and count on my mercy, eh?" Teach kept a straight face for a full ten-seconds before he succumbed to a throaty laugh."

"Shall I throw up the Roger?" Martin asked.

"Immediately," Teach replied. The design of his pirate flag was genius, he had to admit. Upon the traditional black field, stood a horned skeleton holding an hourglass in one hand; in the other, a spear pointing to a heart and three droplets of blood. Genius. Too bad the designer Hans Acsriot had tried to charge extra for the flag—*the greedy buffoon!*

Teach had made short work of the man, fashioning a full set of cutlery from his bleached bones. And…he'd kept the flag too.

"Let the Roger fly!" Teach cried lustily. "Show our prey they've sailed into the wrong harbor. Ocracoke belongs to Blackbeard!"

* * * * * * * *

"At last!" Master Gabriel thundered. "Kaylie Keaton, foolish, foolish, way-too-powerful-for-your-own-good girl! Do you have any idea what I've been going through to pull you out of…of, well, whatever it was you did to yourself?"

Kaylie sat up on her bed, knocking over the books on her bedside table. She blinked up at her Dreamtreading commander. "I'm…I'm home?"

Master Gabriel reached up and tugged the corners of his beard. "Stars and thunder! Yes, you're home…thanks to me. Don't you ever do that again!"

"Do what?"

"Whatever it was that made you go away."

"Oh," Kaylie replied, yawning and stretching. "Oh, that. I didn't know I could do that."

"Now you do, so let this be the only time."

"Okay, Gabe," Kaylie replied. "But one good thing is I got to see Cat and Anne get married—at last!"

"What?"

"Nevermind," Kaylie said. She flopped back onto her bed and closed her eyes.

Master Gabriel harrumphed and said, "I will take that as both a 'thank you' and a 'goodbye.' And I will take my leave."

Kaylie heard the wind chime music of Master Gabriel's departure, but it failed to draw her out of her thoughts. "Oh," she whispered drowsily. "I can't wait to tell Amy about the wedding…"

Many thoughts and images lapped at Kaylie's mind like waves on the bow of *The Bruce*. She thought of Hopper and those adorable blue eyes. She thought about Cat and Anne's long-awaited kiss—and that definitely didn't disappoint.

But most of all, she remembered an island set with jewels that glimmered like stars. All those precious gems, an incalculable fortune really, and yet…for one desperate man, the riches hadn't mattered. What mattered to him was knowing—finally understanding—that the God who spun the universe into existence cared enough about one horribly wicked man to bring him to an island of stars and show him roses, one last time.

The End

ABOUT THE AUTHOR

Wayne Thomas Batson was born in Seabrook, MD in 1968. He had an adventurous childhood and adolescence that included: building forts in the woods, crabbing and crayfishing in bays, ponds, and bayous, playing lead guitar in a heavy metal band, and teaching tennis lessons at the local recreation center. He attended Gabriel DuVal Senior High School where he wrote for the school's newspaper and literary magazine. He was voted "Most Talented" in his senior year, and wrote this for his Yearbook Senior Goal: "To become a published author." Little did he know that God had even greater plans.

Having successfully completed the rigorous Holmes English Literature Curriculum, Batson graduated from the University of Maryland, College Park in 1991 with a BA in English and Secondary Education. In 1996, he earned a graduate degree in Counseling and has continued his studies with 36 credit hours of graduate-level Reading courses.

Wayne Thomas Batson has spent the last twenty-four years teaching Reading and English to middle school students. He pioneered the active instruction of Strategic Reading in Anne Arundel County. Most recently, he helped develop the Challenge Reading Curriculum for advanced readers in Howard County, Maryland. Wayne Thomas Batson lives in Eldersburg with his extraordinary wife of 21 years and his four amazing (and challenging) teenage children.

Batson's writing career began in 2005 with the publication of fantasy epic, *The Door Within*. Since then, *The Door Within*, *The Final Storm*, *Isle of Swords*, and *Isle of Fire* have all appeared on the CBA Young Adult Bestseller List, including #2 for *The Final Storm* Fall 2007. To date, Batson has penned or coauthored seventeen novels and has sold well over half a million copies.

Batson's works have garnered many awards and nominations including: Mom's Choice, Cybil, Lamplighter, Silver Moonbeam, ACFW Book of the Year, and The Clive Staples Award. Mr. Batson and Isle of Swords, his pirate adventure novel, were featured on the front page of The Washington Post, and he was interviewed live on Fox's nationally televised morning show. But most importantly, all of Batson's works are "student approved," meaning that, over the years, the middle school kids in his classes have given each novel a rigorous critique and enthusiastic thumbs up.

Wayne Thomas Batson gives thanks to God for the abundant life he's been given. He continues to write for the kids he cares so deeply about because he believes that, on a deep level, we all long for another world and yearn to do something important.

Acknowledgments:

In Loving Memory of…

Thomas Charles Batson, my Dad.
1929 - 2015
Losing you this year broke my heart, but not my spirit. Your love of good books and ever-present example helped me to know that my endeavors as a writer are worth something, that stories do, in fact, matter. I miss you, Dad, and I can't wait to see you again in heaven and share all the new books with you.

Olin Andrew Dovel, my Pop.
1931 - 2016
It didn't seem fair that, less than four months after losing my father, my wife Mary Lu lost her father too. But through it all, God has been near. Pop, you were as good a man as any I've known. You've left behind a powerful legacy and a challenge to serve others first, just like Christ commanded.

I, Wayne Thomas Batson, do hereby acknowledge that the follow-ing remarkable people invested great love, energy, sacrifice, and kindnesses in ways that I will never be able to repay. Isle of Stars, like all my novels, couldn't have happened without your support and presence in my life. To you, I offer these simple thanks:

Mary Lu Batson: Gorgeous wife, best friend, co-dreamer, and life-mate——to you I offer the greatest human thanks. You committed your life to me, a rare thing these days, and extraordinarily precious to me. Navigating life with four teenagers, teaching, and trying to be a writer would be absolutely impossible without your fantastic support.

Daughter Kayla: your passion and initiative, dreams and drive to help others are nothing short of inspiring. Love you, K-doodle!

Son Tommy: You are a tender warrior, my son. I love the joy you find in God's creation, everything from noticing the gold light before dusk or the smell of woodsmoke on a chill evening. You are a constant reminder to me that God's richest blessings are neverending.

Son Bryce: You are the quiet strength, my son. I love the way you become a student of what inspires you, learning every facet and detail, and then EXPLODE into action. You are committed to excellence. May God use you to do great things.

Daughter Rachel: upon you, God has also placed His creative touch. You are a teacher and a storyteller, a singer and songwriter. I am thankful for the bubbly life you inject into every day. You have a heart full of love to give, and I'm grateful to shepherd you…for a little while.

Mom Batson: I don't know how else to thank you. You gave up 45+ years of your life to directly or indirectly help me be a better son, friend, man, employee, writer, and husband. Thank you!

Mom Dovel: you gave me your daughter and much love besides. Thank you!

Leslie, Jeff, Brian, Edward, Andy, Diana, your spouses, significant others, families, and friends——thank you for creating a landscape of adventure. It is no small thing to be able to raise a sword with such as you.

Doug & Chris, Dave & Heather, ChrisH, Dawn, Dan & Tracey, Warren & Marilyn, Todd W., Alex and Noelle, Alaina, Amanda, Susan, Greg, and all friends past and present: I can't thank you enough for the camaraderie and adventures. May there be many, many more.

Folly Quarter Dreamers: **Erin, Kirsten, Julie, Regina, Barb, Sherrie, Dreia, Lindsay, Susan, Jenny, and Courtney**——you are one amazing group of teachers! Verily, to you I cry out in a loud voice: Deer!

Students Present and Past: you have no idea what precious blessings you are to me and the world. Pip-pip Cheerio!

Sir Gregg of Wooding: agent and friend. Thanks for being among the first to believe in my stories. It is an honor to know you, my friend.

Laura G. Johnson: You are an amazing editor. Thanks for chipping away the chaff so that Isle of Stars could emerge.

Thomas Nelson / Harper Collins & AMG International: you opened the doors of publishing for me. Thank you for the long and incredible ride.

Christopher Hopper——The disciples told Jesus, "We have left all to follow you. What shall we have?" The Lord replied, "Truly I tell you, no one who has left home or wife or brothers or sisters or parents or children for the sake of the kingdom of God will fail to receive many times as much in this age, and in the age to come eternal life." God is true to His word. He linked us in friendship, and I'm grateful. How many O-dark-thirty writing sessions have we shared? How many laughs? Thanks for your friendship, bro. Through airships, flatulent barrister gnomes, spiders, and much more—it has been an honor to ride together. Right™.

Special thanks to **Oscar's in Eldersburg** for being the authentic "Cheers" for me and my family. **Ralph**, you are Da Man!

Cameron Strauss and Family for having my back (in game and out). Thanks also for the town of Avalynn. Beautiful.

Special Thanks to **Nikki Decker** and **Brett Farris** for help with the series name.

To My Guild Family: Bud, Candy, Danley, Cam, Lisa, Chris, Chris, Kimi, Kevin, and Angie: SotB, salute!

My Army of Faithful Online Reader Friends:
• Laura Mary Firemel • Aaron Russell • Ryan Paige Howard • Andrew Bergk • JT Wilt • Gracie Wilt • Tom Wilt • Kaysie Wilt • Mimi Lincicome Wilt • Cameron Strauss and Family • Elizabeth Liberty Lewis • Kaleb Kramer • Ethan Park • Nikita Maves • LoriAnn Weldon • Kathleen Fleeger Edwards • Noah Cutting • Josh Vallance • Kaye Whitney • Addy Buxton • Brian McBride • Rachel O'Malley Brown • Brent Bourgoin • Chris Deanne • Rachel Herriman • Ashton Poole • Lindsay Renea • Brent Ammann • Morgan Babbage • Elizabeth

Hornberger • Jadi Verdin • Jay Goebel • Declan Ross (You know who you are!)

PATREON Patrons: The following people have generously covenanted to support me financially as I continue to seek to serve God and readers by creating the highest quality fiction without sacrificing Christian integrity. Their monthly support enables me to publish more titles, more often, and at lower prices that would ordinarily be required. Cover art (front, back, spine,) is expensive. Interior design is expensive. Editors and proofreaders can be expensive as well. Patreon Patrons, through their monthly support, are countering those costs. My wife, family, and I cannot thank you enough for supporting this mission. Never alone.

Ama Lane

Josiah Mann

Shane Kent

The Starr Family

Michael Harper

Sam Jenne

Christopher Abbott

Christopher Hopper

Laure Hittle

Elizabeth Hornberger

Bryce Spitzer

Eric Guglielmo

Christian Humbert

Chris Harvey

Stephen Larson

Erin Primrose

Brionna Wheaton

Matt Toews

David Larson

Abigail Geiger

Kaylin Calvert

Ruth Geiger

Rebecca Abrams

Ariel Ramey

Cody Pennington

Arikabart Bartholomew

Ryan Paige Howard

Gavin Sullivan

Sir Ethan

Rebekah Main

Logan Brown

Clinton McDonald

Liane Agro & Hannah

Hello, Reader!

I'm Wayne Thomas Batson. I hope you've enjoyed Isle of Stars. Please read on to learn about a great opportunity for you to be a Patron of the Arts and make sure that more stories like this one are possible.

I'm a Christian, an artist, an author, a teacher, a husband, Dad, and friend. I've published 15 books since 2005, several of which became bestsellers in Young Adult niche markets. But the publishing world has changed. Authors no longer have to accept the pittance royalties that legacy publishers offer. We can step out on our own. We can write the stories that make our hearts leap and our imaginations thrum. We can write the stories our readers ask for and maybe even a few stories we all need. But being on our own means a ton of money up front. Cover art, interior design, editing—all come out of pocket. No easy thing for a father of four teenagers, several of whom are entering college age.

Enter Patreon

Patreon is a beautiful thing. It harkens back to Renaissance times when patrons would monetarily support the artists they loved. I'm hoping to be a part of a new Renaissance, one that prompts Christian artists to again lead the way by being excellent at their craft, not shallow and preachy. Would you consider supporting my work with a monthly pledge of any amount? If so, click below:

www.patreon.com/WayneThomasBatson

Other Books by Wayne Thomas Batson…

The Door Within
A secret hidden in his Grandfather's basement sends teenager Aidan Thomas on the adventure of a lifetime. *Dragons Included.*

Rise of the Wyrm Lord
Antoinette Lynn Reed is headstrong, bright, and ridiculously good at martial arts. But will it be enough to overcome a legendary, shapeshifting creature? *Knights Assembly Required.*

The Final Storm
Aidan, Antoinette, and Robby discover that there are some enemies that even the stone walls of Alleble cannot protect against. If anyone will survive the final storm, the cost will be great.
Believe Only As Directed.

Isle of Swords
Three clues: a sparkling green jewel, a rusty iron cross, and a lock of red hair lead a young man and a feared pirate's daughter on a quest for his identity, as well as, a legendary treasure. *For Piratical Use Only.*

Isle of Fire
What happens when bloodthirsty pirates and flame- throwing Vikings join forces? Declan Ross, his fiery daughter Anne, and her friend Griffin "Cat" Thorne will find out in this high seas adventure.
May Explode If Read Improperly.

Isle of Stars
The wedding of Griffin "Cat" Thorne and Anne Ross is on! Or is it? Captain Tobias Dredd, the infamous pirate "Toby Scratch," has been

scouring the South Pacific, searching for Father Carroll, a member of the clandestine holy warriors known only as The Brethren. When Dredd's ship, The Red Corsair, levels a Brethren monastery, Declan Ross and the crew of The Robert Bruce are called upon to pursue Father Carroll and maintain his safety at all costs. The hunt for Father Carroll is on between Ross and Dredd. At stake: the lives of everyone involved and a treasure worth three times the world. For Father Carroll alone knows the location of The Isle of Stars, and he knows its secrets. * *Beware of Falling Roses.*

Curse of the Spider King

Tommy, Kat, and a cast of five other teenagers have two things in common: 1) they all seem to be developing superhuman powers and 2) they are all being stalked by dark, trenchcoated figures with fiery eyes. One wrong move and any of the teens could be caught in the web of The Spider King. *Drefids May Be Closer Than They Appear.*

Venom and Song

The Seven Elven teens are whisked away to Whitehall Castle where they'll be trained as elite Vexbane soldiers. But without learning the secret of the Rainsong, they have no hope against the Spider King. *Elven Personnel Only.*

The Tide of Unmaking

Seven years have passed since the Lords of Berinfell - Tommy, Kat, Jimmy, Johnny, Autumn and Kiri Lee - watched the horror of Vesper Crag wash away, as well as their fallen kinsman, Jett Green. But with Grimwarden in exile, the realm of Berinfell finds itself ill-equipped to weather the coming storms. A consuming terror appears on the horizon: an unstoppable force that threatens to devour all creation and all hope. Nations will crumble, loyalties will be tested, and even the might of Berinfell's Lords may not be enough to stem The Tide of Unmaking. *No Admittance Except on World-Saving Business*

Battle for Cannibal Island (2012)

It's 1852 and cousins Patrick and Beth sail to Fiji on the *HMS Calliope* under the command of Captain James E. Home. They arrive at the islands to find that the Christian Fijians are at war with the non-Christian Fijians. Missionary James Calvert is trying to make peace and suggests that the captain allow peace negotiations on board the British vessel. Patrick and Beth learn about sacrificial living when they observe Calvert's determination to live on Fiji despite the dangers and impoverished conditions and that he is willing to risk his life to live as Jesus would. **Keep Head Protected at All Times.*

Hunt for the Devil's Dragon (2013)

If you're brave, follow cousins Beth and Patrick to Libya in the 13th century. The town of Silene is being terrorized by a vicious animal that is eating livestock. The townspeople believe it's a dragon sent by the devil. In order to appease the beast, the people believe they must offer a human sacrifice   a young girl named Sabra. When Beth tries to help Sabra escape, she too is tied up as an offering for the dragon. Meanwhile, Patrick and a new friend named Hazi join Georgius, a Roman knight who is serving in Africa to keep peace. Georgius decides to find the dragon and kill it. Georgius's plans go awry when Beth and Sabra beg him not to kill the dragon. The girls know the true secret of Silene the dragon isn't its worst enemy.
*Monsters in Mirror May be Larger than they Seem.

Sword in the Stars (Fall 2016)

The wise and powerful Shepherds of Myriad are hearing dangerous voices on the wind. A washed up former assassin and the legend he believes may not be enough to stop a jealous king from unleashing a world-ending war. **Sword Where Prohibited.*

The Errant King (Fall 2016)

Ariana wants nothing more than to escape the nightmares of her past. High King Lochlan wants nothing more than to escape the dreary prospects of his future. But when ancient, legendary creatures attack from east and west, trapping Ariana and Lochlan in the middle, the past and future are in jeopardy for all. *Side Effects Include: Insomnia, Bouts of Dread, and Spontaneous Dueling.*

Mirror of Souls (Fall 2016)
King Lochlan is in exile. Heroes of Myriad's past are presumed dead. A scattered remnant army must evade Morlan's overwhelming Dark Shepherds and Cythraul's Bone Ministers. And, as the Convergence ticks closer, all will come to fear and dread. For something else is about to return from across the Dark Sea. *Do Not Disturb Things Worse Than Dragons.*

Dreamtreaders
Fourteen-year-old Archer Keaton discovers that dreams are much more than they seem. And nightmares? Worse still. Called upon to join the powerful Dreamtreader Order, Archer must face not just his own fears but those of every man, woman, and child living on earth. *Dreamtread for a Limited Time Only.*

Search for the Shadow Key
Betrayed by a friend, Archer Keaton must confront a new Lord of Nightmares. The fabric of the Dream Realm is fraying, and a breach is imminent. Two worlds threatening to collide, Archer makes an ill-advised deal with Bezeal, launching a series of devastating consequences. *Do Not Feed the Nightmare Hounds.*

War for the Waking World
When the Dream and Waking Realms merge, the chaos of unbridled imagination begins to tear everything apart. Archer Keaton is arrested and due to stand trial before the Master of All Dreamtreaders. The fate

of worlds rests in the hands of Archer's prodigy little sister, Kaylie and the Nick Bushman, the Dreamtreader from Down Under. The secret of the Wind Maiden is exposed at last, and there are subtle hints that a mischievous little rogue might turn out to be the most perilous villain of all. *Don't Drink the Water, Especially if it Contains Gort.*

GHOST

John Spector, aka GHOST, isn't your ordinary investigator.

He carries a shiny badge, a billfold ID, and a mysterious silver suitcase. His mission? Seek the forgotten ones, the abandoned ones, the ones no one else can or will help. Visit blunt force trauma upon the world's blackest souls and deny the devil his day by any means necessary. And never stop. Never.

For more than a decade, the "Smiling Jack" killer has been posting photos of his victims on the Web, daring anyone to catch him, daring anyone to care. But when no missing person files match and no victims are ever found, the FBI closes the case.

Years later, a digital camera washes up on shore, and GHOST finds it. Each macabre photo becomes a clue that will lead GHOST and FBI Special Agent Deanna Rezvani on the trail of one of the most diabolical killers of this world...or beyond.

Warning: this product may contain traces of terror, death, and hope.

NOTE: GHOST is intended for mature reading audiences. The appropriate reader age is: 16+

Short Reads (10,000 to 25,000 words) by Wayne Thomas Batson…

The Blackwood (a Door Within Tale)
Nock and Mallik are on the trail of something wicked lurking in
Yewland's famed forest. *Authorized Door Within Readers Only*

The Misadventures of Strylun and Xerk
What happens when Myriad's two most famous bounty hunters are
each given the charge to arrest the other? Bad things. And funny.
War Hammer Included.

Forget Me Not
If a strange old man warns you not to enter a certain part of his vast
garden, you should stay far away. But Lisa and her college friends
don't listen, tumbling into the war between the Hemlocks and the
Broadleaves. *Forests Subject to Change*

Law of the Land
Do this. Don't do that.
Twelve-year-old Jeremy Townsend is sick of rules. Sick of being told
what to do. Sick of being punished. But that's his life. That is until
Jeremy follows a seldom trodden path in the woods and plummets into
the world of Y'Chrana. In Y'Chrana, there are no rules. Stay up all
night. Sleep all day. Eat whatever you want…all the time. It's a dream
come true. But Jeremy's Y'Chranian friend Neil is hiding something.
And everything isn't as it seems. *Living in a Lawless Land Can be
Hazardous to Your Health*

Storms Captured

Before he wrote fantasy and adventure novels, he was a poet. Into each person's lifetime, storms will come. Through wit and verse, the author explores the vital issued of heart and mind. *For a Limited Rhyme Only*

The Dragon in My Closet

When 16 year-old Cassandra McKellen brings a special keepsake home from the Renaissance Festival, she has no idea how special it is indeed. Awakened in the middle of the night by scratching sounds and eerie flickers of light, Cassandra realizes something fantastic is alive and living in her closet. She tries to feed the creature: cat food, lunch meat, and even steak, but discovers that this beast requires a diet of a very different kind. *Crystal Ball Sold Separately.*

The Skeleton Project

Mysterious circumstances lead the FBI to form The Skeleton Project. The most secretive branch of the Bureau, the Skeleton Project searches out the paranormal and supernatural cases that are far beyond the means of regular law enforcement. In these four episodes, you'll meet two of the Skeleton Project's finest agents: obsessive, bend-the-rules Special Agent Oswald "Oz" Pershing and his trigger-happy new partner, Agent Rachel Minnis. Join them as they investigate things that go bump in the night. *No Aliens, No Creatures, No Service.*

Made in United States
Troutdale, OR
09/29/2023

13275517R00098